Hip ski resort + Real live prince =
Best holiday ever!!!

K'WARONTIN

ATTENTION: ORGANIZATIONS AND CORPORATIONS
Most HarperEntertainment books are available at special
quantity discounts for bulk purchases for sales promotions,
premiums, or fund-raising. For information, please call or write:
Special Markets Department, HarperCollins Publishers,
10 East 53rd Street, New York, NY 10022-5299
Telephone: (212) 207-7528 Fax (212) 207-7222

Dream Holiday

By Eliza Willard

HarperEntertainment
An Imprint of HarperCollinsPublishers

A PARACHUTE PRESS BOOK

chapter one

"Wow." Mary-Kate gasped. "Look at the view, Ashley!"

I ran to the living room window. Our rented townhouse—a small, two-story home connected to a row of similar ones—overlooked a forest of pine trees and the Rocky Mountains.

"Isn't it beautiful, girls?" Dad said. He made a big show of taking a deep breath of mountain air. "Two weeks away from the office. No pressures, no deadlines, nothing to worry about but which trail to ski down."

Mom gave him a squeeze. "We could all use a vacation. The girls have been working hard at school, and the day-care center has been a zoo lately. Last week most of the kids came in with colds, and the ones who didn't forgot everything I taught them about sharing."

Dad works for Zone Records, and Mom runs

1

the Sunshine Day Care Center. We rented a town-house at Snowbeam, a beautiful resort in Colorado, for Christmas vacation. The resort had a five-star spa and restaurant, the skiing was the best in the country, and the setting was gorgeous.

I stepped out onto the cedar deck. "Check out the hot tub!" I called.

"Isn't it amazing?" Mary-Kate said, testing the water with her pinkie. "You can sit outside in the freezing air, but the water in the tub is so hot you don't even feel the cold!"

I could just imagine soaking in the tub after a long day of skiing, watching the sun set over the mountains, a mug of hot chocolate in my hand. Ahhh . . .

"And look at this, girls," Dad said, pointing at the backyard. "We can ski right down to the lift from here!"

"That's convenient," Mary-Kate agreed.

"This vacation is going to be all about peace and quiet," Dad said, "and no worries."

"Ow! Louisa, stop pulling my hair!" a child's voice shrieked.

"*You* stop it! Let go!" another child yelled. "Nancy! Make her stop!"

I peered over the fence into the yard next door. There were five red-haired children crowded onto the deck, plus a big, shaggy white dog. Two little girls were pulling each other's hair.

"Give me back my doll!" one girl shouted.

My mom covered her ears. "That sounds just like the day-care center! I can't take it!" She hurried inside.

"It sounds like some rock stars I know, too," Dad added, following her.

But I was curious. I watched over the fence as the sliding door opened and a brown-haired girl about my age stepped out and separated the little girls.

"Louisa, Brigitta, let go," the older girl ordered. "I've got chocolate-chip cookies in the oven, but I'll eat them all myself if you two aren't good! And you know I can do it."

The two girls let go of each other's carrot-colored hair. The sliding door opened again, and out stepped two good-looking adults in the latest skiwear. The woman was blond and the man had a messy thatch of bright red hair just like the kids.

"They must be the parents," I whispered to Mary-Kate.

"Those are some serious ski outfits," she whispered back. "And check out the biceps on him. And her! They must spend all their time working out!"

The parents said something to the kids and squatted to kiss them all. "See you tonight!" the mother called as she and the father left.

One of the kids, a boy of about ten, suddenly spotted Mary-Kate and me. "Hey, look!" he shouted, pointing at us. "Those girls are spying on us!"

Without thinking, I ducked down behind the fence to hide.

"What are you doing? Get back up here." Mary-Kate tugged on my sweater. I felt like an idiot. Why was I hiding?

The brown-haired girl waved to us. "Hey, neighbors," she called.

"Hi," I shouted back. "We weren't spying, I swear. We were just wondering what was going on over there."

"Come on over and see!" the brown-haired girl offered. "It would be nice to talk to someone my own age for a change."

"Hey," the tallest red-haired girl protested. "I'm almost your age."

"You're twelve, Liesl," the brown-haired girl said. "That's not even a teenager yet." She turned to us and added, "Really, come over if you like. The front door is open."

I glanced at Mary-Kate. She shrugged. "Why not?"

We went next door and crowded onto the already crammed deck. "It's the Spy Girls!" the boy cried, grabbing Mary-Kate and me by the wrists. "I've got them!"

4

"Calm down, Freddy," the brown-haired girl said. "And let go of them."

The boy let us go, but he flashed us a grin. "My name is Johansen," he said. "Fred Johansen. And who are you two babes?"

Mary-Kate and I exchanged looks. Was he serious? The kid had to be no more than ten.

The brown-haired girl rolled her eyes. "He's into James Bond," she explained, "but somehow he never gets it quite right. I'm Nancy Lombardi. And these are the Johansens." She patted each red-haired kid in turn as she named them, from oldest to youngest: "Liesl, Friedrich—we call him Fred or Freddy—Brigitta, Louisa, and Kurt."

Liesl was twelve, and Kurt was three. And all the others fell in between—Fred was ten, Brigitta was seven, and Louisa was five.

"I'm their nanny—during Christmas vacation, anyway," Nancy explained. "I usually baby-sit for the Johansens after school, so they asked me to come along and help out on this trip."

"I'm Mary-Kate Olsen, and this is my sister, Ashley," Mary-Kate said.

"Liesl, Brigitta, Kurt . . . those names sound familiar," I said. "Where have I heard them before?"

"*The Sound of Music*," Nancy replied. "Ever see that movie? Mr. and Mrs. Johansen named all their kids after the von Trapp children."

5

"Except they have seven kids in the movie," Liesl said. "We still need a Marta and a Gretel."

"I don't know," Mary-Kate said. "Five seems like plenty to me."

"Trust me, it is," Nancy said. The shaggy white dog waddled through the mob of kids and put his wet nose in my palm. "And this is Soupy."

"Hi, Soupy." I patted him. His paws were muddy and his hair was tangled, but he was a sweet dog. Kurt, the littlest Johansen boy, got down on his hands and knees, crawled up to me, and stuck his face in my other hand, imitating Soupy.

"Kurt, stand up," Nancy scolded. "He likes to do everything Soupy does," she explained. "Oh— my cookies! They're probably ready by now!"

She ran inside. All the kids and Soupy followed her, so Mary-Kate and I went in, too. The house was filled with the smell of fresh-baked cookies.

The kids crowded around the oven as Nancy pulled the cookies out using fancy potholders. Liesl took a carton of milk from the fridge and started filling glasses.

"You guys go play in the living room," Nancy told the kids. "I'll bring the cookies in when they're cool enough to eat, okay?"

The kids toddled out of the kitchen after Liesl, carrying their glasses of milk.

"So, how long are you guys staying?" Nancy

6

asked us. "Will you be here for Christmas?"

I nodded. "We're staying for two weeks."

"Excellent. Snowbeam is so nice at Christmastime. The Johansens come every year. They compete in the Winter Triathlon."

"I read about the triathlon," Mary-Kate said. "Cross-country, downhill, and ski jumping—it sounds like a big deal."

"It is," Nancy said. "They show it on TV and everything. Last year Mrs. Johansen won the women's competition."

"Wow," I said. "She must be a great athlete."

"They both are," Nancy said. "But they're always training, so they're not around much. It's usually just me and the kids."

"Isn't it hard to take care of five kids by yourself?" Mary-Kate asked.

"Not really," Nancy said. "Anyway, there's tons of stuff to do here. There's caroling, and the main lodge is decorated like an old-fashioned Swiss chalet. And then horseback riding, hiking, and skiing, obviously. But the coolest part is the big Christmas Eve party. There's dancing and delicious food, and the waiters wear costumes, and skiers ski down the mountain carrying torches. There are lights everywhere. It's definitely the biggest party of the year. I've heard it's really wonderful."

"You've never been?" Mary-Kate asked.

Nancy shook her head. "Mr. and Mrs. J. go every year. But I have to stay home with the kids. Anyway, it's very exclusive—by invitation only."

"How do you get invited?" I asked.

Nancy shrugged. "Who knows? But you probably would have found an invitation waiting for you in your townhouse if you were invited."

I glanced at Mary-Kate. She shook her head. "I didn't see anything like that."

"Me, neither," I said. "I guess we're not invited."

"Too bad," Nancy said. "Because this year the party should be *really* great, with the prince staying here and everything."

Prince? I hadn't heard anything about a prince staying at Snowbeam.

"Prince?" I asked. "What prince?"

chapter two

"Prince Stephen of Montavan," Nancy said. "He's spending his Christmas vacation at Snowbeam."

Mary-Kate gripped my hand. "Are you kidding me?" she cried. "Prince Stephen is staying here?"

Nancy laughed. "You haven't heard? The whole resort is talking about it."

I grabbed a chair and sank into it. Prince Stephen of Montavan! Here! In this very resort . . . skiing on the same snow as me . . . riding the same lifts . . . snacking at the same snack bars . . .

Everybody knew who Prince Stephen was. His father, King Rudolph, ruled the tiny European kingdom of Montavan. His mother, Queen Anne, was American and a former actress. Prince Stephen was a year older than me, seventeen, and went to Northrup Academy, a prep school in Massachusetts.

"Have you seen him?" I asked Nancy.

"No," she replied. "At least, not that I know of. Nobody knows what he looks like."

"That's right," Mary-Kate said. "His picture has never been published. His parents are terrified of kidnappers."

"But we know his name," I protested. "Maybe we could look up his room number or something and call him."

Nancy snorted. "Are you kidding? I'm sure he's got all kinds of security around him. And anyway, he's not using his real name. I heard he uses a fake name when he goes on vacation to avoid publicity."

"But there must be a way to figure out who he is," I said. "I mean, he's a prince! Doesn't it seem like it should be obvious?"

"I don't know," Mary-Kate said. "His mother's American and he goes to school here, so he doesn't have a foreign accent."

"Believe me, everybody at Snowbeam is trying to pick him out," Nancy said. "Even Mr. and Mrs. J."

I have a gorgeous boyfriend at home, Aaron, and I'm crazy about him, but the idea of meeting a prince was so exciting! I had to meet him. I just had to! How could I spend two weeks so close to a real live prince and not meet him?

"If only we could get invited to the Christmas Eve party somehow," Mary-Kate said. "The prince is sure to be there—and then we could meet him!"

"I like the way you think, Mary-Kate," I said. "But Christmas Eve is more than a week away. Our vacation will be half over by then! I don't want to wait that long. If we could make friends with the prince before the party, he could bring us with him as his guests!"

"You're both dreaming," Nancy said. "How are you going to get invited to the party? And how are you going to meet the prince if you can't figure out who he is?"

"I don't know," I said. "But there's got to be a way."

"Look, it's a beautiful afternoon," Mary-Kate said. "Why don't we hit the slopes?"

"Good idea," Nancy said. "I'll bundle up the kids and meet you outside in half an hour."

"Sounds good," I said. "Who knows—while we're out there, maybe we'll run into Prince Stephen!"

❁

"Maybe that's the prince," Ashley said. We were riding the lift high over the slopes. Below us, a skier struggled down a steep, bumpy hill.

"How can you tell from here?" I asked her. "I can't even tell if it's a guy or a girl."

Ashley shrugged. "I'm just guessing," she admitted.

We'd dropped off the three littlest Johansens

at the Kinder-ski Center, a kind of skiing day care. Then Ashley, Nancy, Liesl, Fred, and I hit the intermediate runs.

"Is that the prince?" Ashley pointed at a guy in the lift ahead of us.

"No, Ashley, that's Fred," I reminded her. The lifts seated four, so Fred and Nancy rode ahead of us. We sat with Liesl.

"Ashley, if you don't stop saying that, I'm going to ski off a cliff," Liesl snapped.

"Sorry," Ashley said. "It's just so exciting! One of these people is probably Prince Stephen. All we have to do is guess which one."

We reached the top of the hill and skied off the lift. Liesl and Fred schussed like experts. "They're all jocks," Nancy said. "They take after their parents."

Fred started humming the James Bond theme music. "Nancy, come on," he said. "The evil Dr. No has sent his ski snipers after us." He pointed at Liesl and shouted, "There's one now!"

Still humming the music, he darted down the slope.

"Eat my dust!" Liesl shouted as she sped down the mountain and passed Fred.

"Be careful!" Nancy called after them. "Wait for me at lift number seven!"

Two men in black ski outfits, their faces completely covered by ski masks and goggles, skied past us.

"Do you think one of those guys is him?" Ashley said.

I rolled my eyes. "Ashley, please. I'll race you to the lift!"

I pushed off with my poles and glided down the hill. It was a perfect winter day. The sun sparkled on the snow. I heard nothing but the wind rushing past my ears. Well, that and Ashley's voice echoing in my head: *Is that the prince? Is that the prince?*

As I watched the skiers around me I had to admit that Snowbeam drew a pretty fancy crowd. Most people had the latest and most expensive high-tech ski gear. And the mountain was crawling with good-looking guys.

Liesl and Fred were waiting for us at the lift line. "I'm glad to see you made it back alive, ladies," Fred said in his James Bond voice. Liesl just snorted and said, "Slowpokes."

We joined the long lift line. Up ahead of us I noticed two guys talking and joking around. They weren't wearing hats and their goggles were propped on top of their heads, so I could see their faces well.

One guy was kind of skinny and small with soft, mousy brown hair. It was the other guy who took my breath away.

He was tall and muscular, with short blond hair mussed by the wind. His eyes were ice blue and his face was handsome, but not in a stuck-up way. His smile was warm and open. He was gorgeous.

"Oh, wow," I said under my breath.

Ashley followed my gaze and spotted the cute guy. "Hey," she said. "Maybe *that's* the—"

I clapped a hand over her mouth. "Don't say it!" I warned. "It's not the prince. It's just the cutest guy I have ever seen in my whole entire life."

"He is pretty stunning," Nancy agreed. "He couldn't be that gorgeous *and* a prince, right? I mean, how could anybody be that lucky?"

"It's not impossible," Ashley insisted. "Look at Prince William."

"You have a point," Nancy said.

"I don't care if he's a prince or a garbageman," I said. "I'm going to meet that guy."

The lift came, and the two guys got on and rode up the mountain. We were six lift chairs behind them.

"We'll never catch up to them," Nancy said. "By the time we get off the lift, they'll be back down here, ready to get on again."

"Maybe they're slow skiers," I offered, though I doubted it. Nancy was right. By the time we reached the top of the slope, the cute blond guy was long gone. And I didn't see him the rest of the afternoon. Not that I didn't try. While Ashley kept her eyes peeled for the prince, I looked and looked for that cute blond guy. Or the C.B.G., as I started to think of him.

"Whew! I'm beat," Nancy said. "Let's quit for the day. I've got to go pick up the little squirts before Kinder-ski closes."

"One more run, Nancy? Oh, please?" Liesl begged.

Nancy shook her head. She wasn't quite as strong a skier as the rest of us. Even the kids had more experience than she did.

"It's time to go home," she told them. "Your parents will be back for supper soon."

"Aww." Fred and Liesl groaned.

We took off our skis and trooped into the lodge. Nancy went off to pick up the little kids. Ashley and I treated Liesl and Fred to hot chocolate while we waited.

"Mary-Kate, look at that." Ashley nudged me. I was expecting to see yet another teenage boy that Ashley was certain was the prince. But instead I saw a brightly colored poster. TEEN PARTY TONIGHT AT THRASHERS IN THE MAIN LODGE. DJ, DANCING, FOOD, AND MORE! THE FUN BEGINS AT 8 P.M.

Hmmm, I thought. *A party. Maybe the cute blond guy will be there!* "Want to go?" I asked Ashley.

"Definitely," she said. "Maybe the prince will be there!"

"That would be cool," I said. But I was much more interested in the C.B.G.

"Did you girls have fun this afternoon?" Mom asked at dinner that night.

Mary-Kate speared some salad with her fork and nodded. "The skiing is great here," she said. "We didn't see you on the slopes."

"We decided to start our vacation off with a good long nap," Dad said. "Tomorrow we'll be fresh and ready to rumble."

"I heard something interesting at the ski shop today," Mom added. "Did you girls know that the Prince of Montavan is here? I mean, right here at Snowbeam!"

"Nancy from next door told us," Mary-Kate said. "Ashley thought every guy between the ages of six and fifty was the prince."

"Did you find out anything about him, Mom?" I asked. "I mean, did you hear any rumors or any hints about what he looks like? Anything?"

"Well," Mom said, "the cashier at the ski shop said she heard he was very handsome."

"Yes, but what does he look like, exactly?" I asked impatiently. "Tall, short? Dark, blond?"

"I heard he's the most gorgeous boy who ever

lived," Dad teased. "If only his parents would let someone take his picture, he'd be a Calvin Klein underwear model."

Mary-Kate laughed. "Come on, Dad, admit it," she said. "If you had a chance to meet Prince Stephen, you'd jump at it."

"I suppose," Dad said. "But I wouldn't go out on a date with him."

Mom rolled her eyes. "Just ignore him, girls. You know how goofy he gets on vacation."

"So what about it, Mom?" I asked. "Did you get any more details?"

"Well, the cashier didn't know exactly what he looks like. But she said that she heard every member of the royal family has some jewelry with the royal seal on it. A pendant, a ring, something like that."

"It's not going to be easy to spot royal jewelry under ski parkas and gloves," Mary-Kate said. "You'll have to use your X-ray vision, Ashley."

I gave her a "very funny" smirk. "I won't need X-ray vision," I said. "Nobody will be wearing ski gloves at the party tonight!"

❀

"This place is packed," Ashley shouted over the dance music. Thrashers, the club in the main lodge, was dark and crowded.

"Check out the snowboarders' convention over

there," Nancy said. A pack of long-haired dudes still in their outdoor gear hung together in a corner.

"Funny how they look just like the surfers back home," I said.

"I think some of them *are* the surfers from back home," Ashley said.

"Do you think the prince is into boarding?" Nancy asked.

"I bet he's a skier," Ashley said. "It's more European."

Ashley scanned the crowd. She was back on her prince hunt. I waited for my eyes to adjust to the darkness and flashing lights, and then I searched the crowd, too. Not for the prince, but for the C.B.G. I just couldn't get him out of my mind.

"I've never seen so many cute guys in one room," Nancy said, "and hardly any girls! There must be two guys for every girl here."

Maybe not quite that many, but still, we were outnumbered for a change. And we didn't mind it a bit.

Someone tapped me on the shoulder. "Hi. Want to dance?" A blocky soccer-player type with curly brown hair was smiling at me. Not the guy I was looking for, but he seemed nice enough. Ashley gave me a nudge.

"Go ahead," she whispered. "Why not?"

"All right," I agreed, and followed the guy out onto the dance floor.

"I'm Carlo," the guy told me.

"Mary-Kate," I said back. We grooved to a hip-hop beat. He was a funny dancer—not the least bit shy. And not coordinated, either. But he was having a good time.

Something flashed in the light as we danced. I slowed down to see what it was. A ring! Carlo was wearing a ring.

Interesting, I thought. How many guys do you know who wear rings? Not too many.

I watched Carlo more closely. Could his ring be a royal seal? Could he be the prince?

I don't know, I thought as he squatted to the floor, spun around, and jumped up again. Would Prince Stephen look like a soccer jock? Would he be such a dorky dancer?

Why not? I decided. *After all, he goes to an East Coast prep school.* Lots of those boys played soccer. And did being born royal give you some kind of magic dancing gene? Unlikely.

I spun around, facing the entrance to the club. And then I saw him. Cute Blond Guy! He was leaning against the wall, talking to another guy.

I turned back to face Carlo. I was dying to go up to the C.B.G. and talk to him. But I couldn't abandon Carlo in the middle of a dance. It would be rude.

When will this stupid song be over? I fretted. Why did the DJ have to play the extended dance mix?

I spun around every once in a while to get a glimpse of the C.B.G. For a second I thought I lost him, but then I spotted him getting a drink.

The song ended. Finally! Another song started, and Carlo kept dancing. But I thanked him and told him I had to run and catch up with a friend.

"Catch you later," he said.

I hurried toward the bar, but the C.B.G. wasn't there. Oh, no! He was heading for the door. He was leaving!

I dashed for the door. I had to catch him. But Ashley and Nancy blocked my path.

"Mary-Kate!" Ashley gasped. "We found him! We found the prince!"

chapter three

"We think I've spotted him!" Nancy cried.

"It's got to be him," Ashley added.

"Great," I said. "I'll be right back." I pushed past them and hurried to the door. The C.B.G. was gone. I ran outside into the lobby. No sign of him.

I went back inside the disco. "What was that all about?" Ashley asked.

"I saw the Cute Blond Guy," I told her. "But I lost him."

Ashley waved this away. "You can see some regular blond guy anytime. This is Prince Stephen we're talking about!"

"Where is he?" I asked. "How do you know it's him?"

"We overheard him talking to one of his friends," Nancy explained. "About *Montavan*. He said something like 'The last time I was in Montavan it rained for three days straight.' I mean, how many guys do you know who spend a lot of time in Montavan?"

"That's true," I said, but that glint of gold flashed in my mind and I remembered Carlo's ring. I was so excited to see the C.B.G., I'd forgotten all about it. "But I think *I* might have found the prince," I said. "That guy I was dancing with? He's wearing a gold ring!"

"Was it the royal seal?" Ashley asked.

"I don't know," I said. "What does the royal seal look like?"

Ashley shrugged. "I have no idea. But I think I'd know it if I saw it. You go back and get a better look at it. We'll go talk to Mr. Rain-in-Montavan and see what we can find out."

"Okay." If I couldn't meet my C.B.G., I might as well join Ashley's prince hunt.

I found Carlo at the bar, gulping down a bottle of water. "Hey, you're back," he said, smiling. "I'm almost ready to hit the dance floor again."

"I'm still recovering from that last song," I said. I leaned across the bar and ordered a soda. Carlo's ring caught the light again.

"That's an interesting-looking ring," I said to him. "May I see it?"

"Sure." He held his hand out.

I studied the ring in a spotlight. It did look like some kind of seal. It had a lion's head, a hammer, and some other strange symbols on it.

"What is it?" I asked. "I mean, what do all these symbols mean?"

"The lion is for courage," Carlo said. "The hammer stands for hard work, and these symbols stand for *Delta Tau Delta*."

"*Delta Tau Delta*? Is that some kind of motto?" I asked.

Carlo shook his head. "No. It's Greek. It's the name of my dad's frat at U.C.L.A."

"Oh. So it's a fraternity ring," I said.

"Yeah," Carlo said. "My dad gave it to me. It doesn't fit him anymore."

Oh, well. Maybe Ashley and Nancy were having better luck.

"Want to dance again?" Carlo asked.

"Thanks, but I've got to find my sister," I told him. "See you later."

❀

"There he is," Nancy whispered, pointing at a tall, slim guy with short black hair. "The guy who mentioned Montavan." He was wearing khakis, a blazer, and an open-necked button-down shirt.

He was sitting on a tall stool next to a stocky, windburned guy, sipping a Pellegrino.

"Let's get closer," I said. "Maybe we'll overhear something else."

Nancy and I moved toward the two guys.

"I can't stay for the race," the black-haired guy said. "I've got to be back at school by the fifth."

"The fifth!" the other guy said. "We get the whole month of January off."

"So do we," said the maybe-prince. "But I row crew. They open the dorms in January just so the crew team can train all month. It's brutal."

"Did you hear that?" I nudged Nancy. "Dorms, crew team . . . He must go to a prep school somewhere. He *could* be the prince!"

"Let's go talk to them," Nancy said.

We strolled up to them as if we were going to order sodas. Nancy beamed at the maybe-prince and said, "Hi."

The maybe-prince smiled back. "Hi, girls. Great skiing today, huh?"

"Definitely," I said. "Um, I'm Ashley, and this is my friend, Nancy."

"I'm Henry, and this is Cody," Maybe-Prince said.

His name is Henry, not Stephen, I thought. *But that's good, because the prince is using a fake name. If he said his name was Stephen, that would mean he probably wasn't the prince!*

"Where are you two from?" Cody asked.

"I'm from Malibu," I replied.

"San Francisco," Nancy said.

"We just met yesterday," I explained. "Our

townhouses are right next door to each other."

"We met on a bike trip through Europe last summer," Henry said.

A bike trip through Europe—good sign or bad? I couldn't decide.

"That sounds like fun," I said. "Which country did you like the best?"

Henry glanced at Cody. "Italy was cool," he said.

"I liked Spain," Cody said.

"We went through France and Montavan, too," Henry added.

"Montavan was a drag," Cody said.

"Yeah, it was pretty, but kind of boring," Henry added.

I glanced at Nancy. The way Henry was talking about Europe didn't sound very princely. Especially the Montavan part.

"Where are you from?" Nancy asked them.

"Texas," Cody said.

"New Jersey," Henry offered.

Now that he mentioned it, I could hear the New Jersey in his accent. Nancy pinched my side. I could tell she was thinking the same thing I was: *No way was this guy the prince.*

Maybe Mary-Kate had better luck, I thought. I spotted her across the room, looking for us.

"There's my sister," I said. "We'd better go. Nice meeting you."

"You, too," Henry said. "See you on the slopes!"

"Any luck?" Mary-Kate asked when we met her near the dance floor.

"No," I said. "You?"

She shook her head. "It was his dad's frat ring."

"Let's get out of here," I said. "We should have known the prince wouldn't be at a teen party."

"He *could* be here," Nancy said. "Maybe we just haven't found him yet."

I looked around at all the guys talking to one another and checking out the girls. It was lame. "If I were a prince, somehow I think I'd find something better to do that this," I said. "Let's go."

❀

"Let's try a double black diamond run today," Ashley suggested the next morning.

"Excellent idea," I agreed.

It was another sparkling day and we were riding the lift together for our first ski run of the morning. We had stuck to the intermediate slopes the day before because Nancy wasn't a very good skier. But she had to stay home with the Johansen kids today.

We got off the lift and headed for a double black diamond—the most advanced run.

"Wow," Ashley gasped, staring down the

mountainside. "That's practically vertical."

"You can do it," I said, and started down the hill. My heart raced and I gulped in the fresh air. What a rush!

"Whew," Ashley said when we reached the bottom.

"Let's go again," I said.

After another run, Ashley convinced me to take a break for hot chocolate. We stopped at a ski-up snack bar surrounded by picnic tables.

Ashley pointed to a good-looking guy taking off his skis. "Do you think that's the prince?"

I rolled my eyes. Not another day of that.

Then I spotted him. He was getting up from one of the picnic tables. The C.B.G.

Jackpot, I thought. He looked even cuter than before. He'd gotten a little sun on his face and the tan made the blue of his eyes even brighter.

"There he is," I said.

"Who?" Ashley asked. "The prince? Where?"

"No, not the prince," I snapped. "The C.B.G.! He's getting back on the lift line. We've got to catch up with him!"

"But I haven't finished my hot chocolate yet!" Ashley complained.

"I'll buy you another one later. Come on!"

I sprang to my feet, splattering hot chocolate on the snow, and shuffled toward the lift line.

Each chairlift held four people. If I could just get next to him in line, we could ride up together. And then he'd have to talk to me. How could he avoid it? We'd be sitting right next to each other.

"Wait for me!" Ashley called.

The C.B.G. and his friend were already in line. Two couples skied in after them.

I wasn't about to let them get in my way. I pushed past the couples so I could be right behind the boys. There was only one group ahead of the boys. They were about to get on the lift. I waved frantically at Ashley to hurry up.

She stumbled past the people waiting in line. "I felt kind of rude cutting in front of all those people," Ashley whispered.

"Shhh," I said. "Here it comes."

We lined ourselves up next to the boys. The chair came behind us and picked us up. We'd made it!

The C.B.G. sat at the far end of the chair. Too bad. His friend was next to me, and Ashley had the left end. The friend was smaller and skinnier than the C.B.G., with short brown hair and a bashful face. He looked a little nerdy, which was funny, because the C.B.G. wasn't nerdy at all.

I waited for the boys to say something, but they didn't. So I took the initiative.

"Hi," I said.

"Hi," both boys said back.

Then nothing. I tried again. "Isn't it a beautiful day?"

"Sure is," said the C.B.G.'s friend.

Another silence. I looked to Ashley for help. She shrugged.

I had to say something. Anything! But what? "Um, do you like skiing?"

I wanted to slap my forehead with my mittened hand. *Do you like skiing?* How could I have been so stupid?

"Well, we're here, right?" the C.B.G. replied.

I laughed nervously. "Yeah, you're right. What a silly question. . . ."

The lift was moving steadily up the hill. We were almost halfway there. I didn't have much time left.

I went for the old standby. "I'm Mary-Kate, and this is my sister, Ashley."

The boys glanced at us and nodded. "Nice to meet you, Mary-Kate and Ashley," the C.B.G. said.

I waited for them to tell us their names, but they didn't. What was wrong with them?

Ashley tried to help. "Have you been to Snowbeam before?" she asked.

At that moment, the lift reached the top of the mountain. We all slid off. The C.B.G. and his friend skied ahead of us. He looked back, waved his pole, and called, "See you around!"

Then they dashed down the mountain.

"I can't believe it," Ashley said. "We got nothing!"

"I'm going to try again," I said. I was determined to get that boy's attention. "Let's catch up to them!"

We sped down the hill after the boys. I thought I'd see them at the first turn, but they were nowhere in sight.

"Where did they go?" Ashley shouted.

"Keep going!" I said.

We were almost at the bottom of the mountain. I could see the lift line ahead of us. There they were! They were getting back in line. I had to catch up with them.

I crouched low, ducking my head against the wind, and skied toward that lift line as fast as I could. I looked up. I was almost there!

I sped up a little more—but I was going too fast. I lost control. My arms flailed and my ski poles went flying.

I crashed to a stop face-first in the snow.

Right in front of the C.B.G.

chapter four

"Are you all right?" the C.B.G. asked. He and his friend helped me to my feet. Ashley skidded to a stop and helped them brush the snow off me.

"Did you hurt yourself, Mary-Kate?" she asked.

"I think I'm okay," I said. *Just totally embarrassed*, I thought.

The C.B.G. started to laugh. "That was a pretty wild fall. Are you sure you're okay?"

I felt my arms and legs and ribs and said, "Everything checks out."

"You'll probably be sore tomorrow," the C.B.G. said. "Want to ride up with us again?"

"Sure," I said, grinning at Ashley. So that's what it took to get his attention—complete humiliation!

"I'm Nate," the friend said. He smiled shyly and shook my hand, then Ashley's.

"I'm Bill," the C.B.G. said, shaking hands, too.

I thought. *I can finally put a name to that
ooking face.*

The lift came, and this time Bill sat next to
me, and Nate sat between me and Ashley.

"Where are you from?" I asked Bill.

"Back East," he said. "How about you?"

"Out West," I replied. "Have you been to Snowbeam before?"

"It's my first time," Bill answered. "It's the
nicest place I've ever skied."

"Have you skied in a lot of other places?" I
asked him.

"Some," he said. "Vermont, Utah, the Alps . . ."

"The Alps must be beautiful," I said.

"They are," Bill said. "But the air feels colder
there. And the slopes are more crowded, at least
where I was."

Nate was quiet while Bill and I talked. I heard
Ashley asking him a few questions but didn't catch
the answers. I was too focused on Bill. Now that
we were up close and talking to him, I liked him
even more.

I got nervous as the lift neared the top of the
mountain. Would Bill ask me to ski with him?
Would I get to spend more time with him?

Our skis slapped the snow as we dismounted.
Bill grinned at me. "Well, maybe we'll see you
around," he said. He and Nate pushed off and skied

away. I was so shocked all I could do was stare after them with my mouth hanging open. Ashley reached over and gently closed my mouth for me.

"I can't believe it," I said. "I finally got to talk to him, and it was nice! Now I'll probably never see him again!"

"You've already seen him three times in two days," Ashley pointed out. "Don't worry. We'll run into him again. Now come on. Let's do another black diamond run."

We started down the slope. We turned a corner past a stand of pine trees. A lone skier stood there, as if he was waiting for someone.

I got closer. It was Bill!

I schussed to a stop. Ashley skied past, grinning. "Hey," he said. "Would you like to go out with me sometime?"

"Sure!" I said, not even bothering to act cool. I gave him my cell-phone number. He took out his cell phone and punched it in.

"Got it," he said. "I'll call you soon! Have a good run!" He sped away to catch up with Nate. I stood watching him, breathless.

Once he was gone, I swooshed down the mountain, shouting, "*Woo hoo!*" into the wind.

❀

"Ow. My muscles are sore already," Mary-Kate said. We had slid into the hot tub at the end of our long day. Nancy was off for the evening and had come over to join us.

"I think I'll spend tomorrow at the spa," Mary-Kate said. "I'm going to be an achy mess in the morning, I can tell."

"Did you take a bad spill?" Nancy asked.

Mary-Kate nodded. "But it was worth it."

"She met a guy," I explained to Nancy.

"The *cutest* guy," Mary-Kate added. "His name is Bill. He asked me out!"

"Hi, girls." Mom stepped out on the deck. "How's the hot tub?"

"Great," Mary-Kate said.

"Did you have fun skiing today?" Mom asked. "Your dad was looking for you practically all afternoon. He was sure he'd spot you somewhere on the slopes."

I laughed. I'd had my eye out for the prince, Mary-Kate had been looking for her C.B.G., and Dad had been looking for us! Everybody seemed to be looking for somebody.

"We were definitely there," I said. "I don't know how you missed us."

"I'm making decaf mocha lattes," Mom said. "How about it? Anybody up for one?"

"I'd love one," Mary-Kate said.

"Me too," Nancy said.

"Me too," I said. "Thanks, Mom."

"Three decaf mocha lattes, coming up." Mom disappeared inside the house.

"Any prince sightings today?" Nancy asked.

"No," I said. "Nothing. I mean, who knows, we could have skied right past him a dozen times. I wish there was a way to figure out what he looks like."

"I keep thinking that I'll take one look at him and just *know*," Nancy said. "It must sound crazy, but I just have that feeling."

"Want to come skiing with me tomorrow?" I asked. "I think Mary-Kate's going to be out of commission."

Mary-Kate nodded. "I need a recovery day."

"I definitely want to go," Nancy said. "I'm off tomorrow."

"Good," I said. "We'll look for the prince some more. And if your sixth sense starts tingling, we'll know we've got him!"

"Let's try that run this time, Ashley," Nancy said the next day. She pointed to an advanced black diamond run.

"Are you sure?" I asked her. "That run is pretty tough."

"I'm positive," Nancy said. "I feel great today. And I'm bored with the intermediate slopes. We've already skied each one three times."

I was bored with them, too, and itching to ski

more advanced runs. "It's really steep," I warned.

"I can handle it," she said. "Besides, we'll never spot the prince if we stay on the intermediate runs. I'm sure he's an advanced skier."

I shrugged. "Okay, let's do it." I started down the Black Diamond run. Nancy followed me. It was a tricky slope, so I zigzagged down it carefully. Suddenly I heard a scream and felt a rush of air blow past me. *Nancy!*

"Ashley, help!" she cried. She whizzed down the mountain, totally out of control!

"Go sideways!" I shouted. "Fall on your butt!" But I don't think she could hear me. She skied straight for a tree. She screamed and dodged the tree, but fell forward, hard.

"Nancy!" I shouted, racing toward her. "Are you all right?"

Nancy groaned and winced with pain. She clutched her right leg.

"I hurt my leg." She moaned. "I think it's broken!"

Oh, no! I thought, panicking. *What am I going to do?*

chapter five

"Can you sit up?" I asked Nancy. Her leg was twisted at a weird angle. It didn't look good.

She shook her head. "I don't think so." Tears welled in her eyes and she was breathing hard. "It really hurts!"

Up ahead, a woman skied toward us. "Help!" I shouted, waving my arms at her. "Emergency!" She stopped.

"What happened?" the woman asked. "Is she all right?"

"She's hurt," I said. "We need the ski patrol. I think she needs a stretcher."

"I'll stop at the next lift and send the ski patrol," the woman promised.

"Thank you," I said.

In a few minutes two ski patrollers—a guy and a girl in their twenties—arrived on a bright yellow snowmobile towing a stretcher. A big

German shepherd trotted along behind it wearing a rescue halter with a red cross on it.

"What happened?" the guy asked.

I explained while he and the girl examined Nancy. "Looks like a bad break," the girl said. "We're taking her to the hospital. I'll call for another snowmobile so you can come with us."

She radioed for another snowmobile to pick me up. It arrived just as they gently settled Nancy on the stretcher. We drove down the hill to a waiting ambulance and then rushed to the hospital.

I sat in the back with Nancy. "You're going to be okay," I told her. She nodded but grimaced in pain.

"Doctor, is she going to be all right?" Mrs. Johansen asked. She and her husband had hurried to the hospital as soon as they heard about the accident. Nancy had been whisked into an emergency room while I waited with them.

"She'll be fine," the doctor said. "It's a broken leg, just as we thought. I reset the bone and put the leg in a cast. She'll have to wear the cast for three months."

"Three months!" Mrs. J. said. "Poor girl."

"She'll need to keep the leg elevated for a while," the doctor added. "And I think she should have a good week or two of bed rest."

"Of course, Doctor," Mr. J. said. "We'll arrange

for her to go home to her parents right away."

"Can we see her?" I asked.

"Right this way." The doctor led us to Nancy's room. I followed the Johansens in.

"I'm so sorry!" Nancy cried when she saw us. "I've ruined everybody's Christmas vacation!"

"Shhh," Mrs. Johansen said. "Don't be silly. The important thing is that you're all right."

"I can't believe I have to go home already." Nancy sniffled. "Ashley, if you find the prince, you have to E-mail me right away."

"I promise," I said.

"What are you going to do?" Nancy asked the Johansens. "What about the kids? Who's going to take care of them?"

"We will," Mr. J. said. "I know it's hard to believe, but we're perfectly capable of taking care of own children."

"But what about the triathlon?" Nancy said. "How can you train if you have to take care of the kids?"

"We'll work something out," Mrs. J. said.

"But you're the defending champion!" Nancy said. "You can't drop out of the race."

Nancy looked upset. I knew she thought she was letting the Johansens down. I couldn't help feeling guilty. It was partly my fault that she got hurt. We never should have skied down that advanced run. I knew she wasn't ready for it.

"Maybe I can help out," I offered. "I could watch the kids sometimes to give you a chance to train."

Mrs. J.'s face lit up. "That would be wonderful, Ashley," she said. "We'd only really need you during our training sessions."

"There are only three sessions left before the triathlon," Mr. Johansen added. "But I'd hate to ask you to give up your vacation time."

"I wouldn't mind, really," I said. "I love kids." And it didn't sound like too much work. Just three training sessions, whatever that was. How long could a training session last?

"Do you really mean it?" Nancy asked.

"We'll try to keep your nanny time to a minimum," Mr. J. promised. "And we'll pay you a full salary, of course."

"Perfect," I said. They all looked so happy, I was glad I could help. And maybe it would be fun!

❀

I dragged myself out of the warm mud bath and headed for the shower. After a long morning at the spa, my sore muscles were as good as new.

I stopped at my locker and checked my cell phone. I had a voice-mail message. Excellent! Maybe Bill had called!

My heart sank as I listened to the message. It

wasn't from Bill. It was from Ashley. And she had bad news. Nancy had fallen and broken her leg!

I felt terrible for Nancy. I thought about her as I showered and got dressed. Ashley said Nancy had to go home to San Francisco and miss the rest of the trip. I knew she must be very upset.

My phone rang. I stared at the number on the screen. I didn't recognize it, and my caller I.D. didn't show the name. I quickly prayed for it to be Bill, then answered it.

"Mary-Kate? This is Bill. The guy you took a snow bath in front of yesterday?"

Yes! He had only waited one day to call. That's a very good sign.

"Hi, Bill," I said. "I'm at the spa. Yesterday I took a snow bath and today I took a mud bath. I think tomorrow I'll try plain old dirt."

He laughed. "Are you busy tomorrow? I mean, after your dirt bath?"

"Not really," I said.

"I thought we could get together, maybe go horseback riding or something like that. What do you think?"

"Sounds great," I said, struggling not to let him hear the excitement in my voice. Horseback riding with Bill! It would be so romantic!

"Good," he said. "I'll meet you at the main lodge at noon tomorrow. That way you can get in a morning of skiing first if you want—okay?"

"That's perfect!" I said. But I knew I wouldn't spend the morning skiing. I needed a few hours to try on every piece of clothing I'd brought with me to find the perfect horseback-riding outfit!

❁

"I made a pan of turkey tetrazzini for the kids' lunch," Mrs. Johansen said the next day. She opened the fridge and showed me the pan of turkey-noodle casserole. "Just bake it in the oven at three hundred and fifty degrees for thirty-five minutes."

I nodded. It was my first day of nannying and Mrs. J. was showing me around and explaining the house rules to me.

"The kids will probably ask you for candy or to take them to McDonald's or something—especially Louisa," Mrs. J. warned. "But I like to watch their diets very carefully. I feed them organic food as much as possible. Once in a while they can have homemade cookies as a treat, but in general I try to limit their sugar intake."

I nodded again. "No problem."

"Good," Mrs. J. said. "Well, I guess that's it for now."

"Let's go, Beth," Mr. J. called from the front door. "We're going to be late for the time trials."

"I'm coming!" She hurried to the front door

and grabbed her jacket. "Good luck, Ashley. We'll be home by six."

"Be good, kids," Mr. J. added. Then they drove off to their training session.

The door closed. I turned around to face five messy red-haired, hazel-eyed kids in their pajamas.

"Well, we might as well start by getting dressed," I said. "Let's go upstairs."

Kurt, the three-year-old, waddled up to me and clutched my leg. I took a step and he clung to me.

"Kurt, please let go of me," I said.

"I love you," he said.

"That's sweet," I answered. "But you've got to let go of my leg, or I won't be able to walk."

"No!" he cried. I tried to take another step. He hung on. I tried to shake him off. Nothing worked.

"Liesl, what should I do?" I asked the oldest girl.

"I don't know," Liesl said. "It's not my problem. You're the nanny. You deal with it." She ran upstairs.

"Okay . . ." I said, and my eyes fell on Fred, the next oldest at ten.

"Ashley, babe, I'll take care of it," Fred said in his weird James-Bond-meets-the-Rugrats voice. His pajamas were printed to look like a tuxedo. He peeled Kurt off my leg. Then he turned Kurt to face Soupy, who lay slobbering on the couch.

"Kurt, Soupy would never cling to Ashley's leg like that," he said. "See Soupy? Why don't you do what Soupy's doing?"

Kurt broke into a grin and ran to the couch, where he curled up and laid his head on his hands just like a dog.

"Problem solved," Fred said.

"Thank you."

Kurt watched Soupy closely. Then he started spitting on the couch.

"Kurt, stop that!" I cried. I looked to Fred for help. "What is he doing?"

"Drooling," Fred explained. "Like Soupy."

I grabbed Kurt and made him sit up. "Sorry, Kurt. No drooling on the couch." I helped him to his feet. "Let's go upstairs and get dressed. Soupy, off the couch." I nudged Soupy to the floor, then led him to the back door and let him outside. Then I took Kurt upstairs with me.

The townhouse had four bedrooms upstairs: one for Mr. and Mrs. J., one for the two boys, one for the three girls, and Nancy's room. Liesl had taken over Nancy's room and made it her own. I popped my head in on my way to the boys' room. Liesl was already dressed, lying on her bed, and listening to music through earphones.

"Everything okay in here?" I asked.

"I'm twelve, you know," Liesl snapped. "I don't

need a baby-sitter." She crossed her arms.

I remembered feeling exactly the same way at twelve. "I know," I told her. "But the younger kids need to be watched. You and I can be friends— and maybe you can help me out if I need it. How's that sound?"

"Okay, I guess," Liesl said.

I smiled. *I'm going to be great at this*, I thought. Then I pushed my luck.

"So, Liesl, will you do me a favor and help Brigitta and Louisa get dressed?" I asked.

She rolled her eyes. "I'm *busy*."

Okay, I thought. *So much for bonding with Liesl.*

"Where is Bessie, where is Bessie?" Brigitta and Louisa sang from the next room. "Bessie messy Bess?"

I peeked in. Brigitta and Louisa were tearing their room apart, pulling their clothes out of every drawer and tossing them on the floor, digging through the closet, jumping on the beds . . . and of course they weren't dressed yet.

"What are you doing?" I asked.

"Looking for my doll, Bessie," Louisa explained. She picked up a box of toys and dumped them on the floor.

"Here she is!" Brigitta came up from under her bed covered in dust bunnies and waving a baby doll dressed in a diaper made out of a paper towel.

"Give it!" Louisa cried, grabbing for the doll.

"Finders keepers!" Brigitta said. "She's mine now!"

"No! She's mine!" Louisa reached for the doll again but missed and hit Brigitta in the arm. I stepped between them before it could turn into an all-out brawl.

"Kurt, whose doll is this?" I asked.

"Mine!" Louisa said.

"Louisa's," Kurt confirmed.

Brigitta didn't protest, so I gave the doll to Louisa. "Get dressed and clean up your room right now," I said. I took Kurt to his room. Fred was already dressed in a neat pair of pants and button-down shirt. He was a funny little-old-mannish boy. I half expected him to be wearing a bow tie.

"Come on, Kurt," I said, taking off his pajamas. "Let's get you dressed quickly before your sisters tear the house apart."

I put Kurt in a cute pair of overalls, then went to check on the girls. They hadn't cleaned up their room, but they were dressed and playing quietly. Good enough for me.

The next couple of hours went quickly. Brigitta and Louisa fought about once every half hour. Kurt kept opening the back door to let Soupy in, and Soupy tracked mud all over the house. I shooed Soupy out and cleaned up the mud, but the place wasn't clean for ten minutes before Kurt let Soupy in again.

"Stop that, Kurt!" I scolded. "Soupy stays outside for now."

Upstairs, another fight broke out between Louisa and Brigitta.

"Ashley, babe, I'll let you in on a secret," Fred said. "Keep Briggy and Louisa apart and they won't fight so much. I'll play a game with the Brigmeister while you keep Louisa busy. What do you say, sweetcakes?"

Listening to Fred talk left my head reeling, so it took me a few seconds to answer.

"Thanks for the advice, Fred," I said. "Sounds like a plan."

Fred went upstairs to play with Brigitta. Louisa brought her doll downstairs to me. I sat Kurt in front of the TV to watch a video. Louisa dragged me into the dining room. We huddled under the table.

"Let's play Baby-sitter," Louisa said. "You be Kurt and I'll be Nancy."

"Okay," I agreed. It sounded like a weird game to me, but whatever.

"Get on the floor and crawl around like a baby," Louisa ordered. "You're Kurt."

"Oh." I crouched on the rug on my hands and knees. Louisa patted my head.

"Good boy, Kurt," she said in a high-pitched voice. I guess that's the way she thought Nancy talked. "I'm Nancy, your baby-sitter. And you have to do whatever I say."

"No, I don't, Nancy," I said in a voice as close to Kurt's as I could get. "I'm a spoiled brat. I do whatever I want."

"Ha, ha. Here's your dolly, Kurt. Now cry like a baby."

I took the doll and sighed. I really didn't want to pretend to cry like a baby.

"Kurt, you *have* to," Louisa ordered. "I'm the boss."

"Wah," I said half-heartedly. "Wah. Wah."

My stomach rumbled and I remembered lunch. Ah-ha! The perfect excuse to get out of this crazy game.

"I'll be right back, Louisa," I said, getting to my feet. "I've just got to put lunch in the oven."

"Get back here!" Louisa shouted. "*I'm* the baby-sitter! *I'm* the one who makes lunch!"

"Just wait one second!" I called. I ran into the kitchen, turned on the oven, and put the pan of turkey tetrazzini in without bothering to preheat. I didn't want to provoke any more yelling from Louisa than I had to.

When I returned to the dining room, Louisa was busy changing Bessie's paper-towel diaper. I glanced toward the TV to check on Kurt. He wasn't there.

"Louisa, where's Kurt?" I asked.

She pointed at me. "You're Kurt. Get back down on the floor."

"No, I mean the real Kurt," I said. "Your brother?"

She shrugged. I stood up and walked into the living room. "Kurt, come back here!" Louisa yelled at me. "I need to change your diaper!" I ignored her. I had to find Kurt.

He wasn't in the kitchen and he wasn't upstairs. I went outside to the backyard. There he was, sitting in a puddle of mud right next to Soupy. He was copying Soupy's position exactly.

What a weird kid, I thought, marching across the yard to get him. "Kurt, get up from there! You're not even wearing a coat!"

I brought him inside to the bathroom to take off his muddy clothes.

"Something smells funny," Kurt said.

I sniffed. He was right—something did smell funny. I sniffed again.

Smoke!

"Oh, no!" I shouted. "Our lunch is burning!"

chapter six

Smoke poured out of the oven. I yanked open the oven door and waved the smoke away. Our lunch had burned to a crisp!

The kids ran into the kitchen to see what was wrong. "What's happening?" Liesl asked. "What's that smell?"

"Our lunch," I told them. I picked up some potholders and pulled out the pan of turkey tetrazzini. It was black and charred on top and smelled terrible.

"Ew, that's our lunch?" Brigitta said. "I don't want to eat that!"

"How did this happen?" I muttered. "I followed the instructions. . . ."

I checked the temperature dial on the oven. It had been turned up to broil. But I was sure I had set it for three hundred and fifty degrees.

"Has somebody been playing with the oven?"

I asked, scanning the kids' faces. Louisa turned away, looking guilty.

"Louisa?" I said.

"I'm Nancy!" She stamped her foot. "It's my job to turn on the oven! Not yours!"

"So you turned up the oven?" I cried. "That's very bad. You've ruined our lunch!"

"Louisa, you know you're not allowed to touch the oven or the stove, ever!" Liesl scolded.

"But I was Nancy!" Louisa protested. "I was supposed to make lunch!"

Liesl glanced at me. "Do you know what she's talking about?"

"Sort of," I said. "But that doesn't make it any less crazy." I opened the window to clear out some of the smoke.

"When's lunch?" Brigitta asked. "I'm hungry."

I glanced back at the oven. The turkey tetrazzini sat ruined on top of the stove.

"Let's see what we've got here." I rummaged through the cabinets. There wasn't much left—not even a jar of peanut butter.

"Get your coats on," I said. "We're going to the supermarket."

❋

"You hungry, Mary-Kate?" Bill asked.

"Starving," I confessed. "But what can we eat?" We'd been riding through the snow-covered woods for over an hour. Neither of us had brought any food.

"Leave it to me," Bill said. In a few minutes I saw a plume of smoke up ahead, and we came to an old German-style inn.

"It's beautiful!" I said. It was like a gingerbread house. The smell of fresh-baked bread and roasting meat poured out of a kitchen window.

Bill dismounted and helped me off my horse. He had arranged everything, from borrowing the horses from the Snowbeam stables to mapping out the best riding trail, and now finding this cute little inn to stop at.

"The manager at Snowbeam told me this place makes great hot cider," Bill said.

We settled at a cozy booth in the corner. "How did you learn to ride so well?" I asked him.

"Oh, I don't know." Bill shrugged. "There were always horses around when I was growing up, I guess. What about you? You're pretty good, too."

"Thanks," I said. "I've always loved horses."

We ordered soup and hot cider. "It must be cool living on the beach all year round," he said. "You can go swimming in the winter and everything?"

"Sure," I said. "It gets chilly once in a while but never cold like it is here."

He grinned. "I'd never get any homework done if I could hang out on the beach every day."

"It's hard," I agreed, "but you get used to it. Sometimes school keeps me so busy I forget the ocean's there."

The waiter brought our hot cider. "What about you?" I asked Bill. "Where are you from?"

"Oh, all over," he said.

I frowned. Most of the time, Bill seemed very open and friendly. But sometimes when I asked him certain questions, his answers were kind of vague. "Well, you said you were from back East when I met you," I prodded.

"Yeah—I live on the East Coast now," he said. "But I grew up all over the place. I'm an army brat."

That explained it. I'd met other kids whose parents were in the military and they all moved around a lot. They seemed almost embarrassed because they didn't really have a hometown.

"Are the girls back East good skiers?" I asked. "I'll bet they don't fall face-first in the snow when they meet you."

"You didn't have to try so hard to get my attention," he said. "I mean, I already noticed you. But the first time we rode the lift together, it was awkward. Nate was sitting next to you, and he can be kind of shy. But I definitely thought you were the cutest girl on the slopes. You look even better with a snow mustache."

A jolt of excitement zipped up my spine. He

liked me! "Thanks. You should see me with a mud mustache."

We drank our hot cider and ate the soup. Everything was delicious. When the bill came, Bill insisted on paying. He opened his wallet and pulled out a credit card. His wallet was only open for a split second, but I caught a glimpse of some kind of ID card. It said "Northrup Academy Parking Permit."

Northrup Academy? Why did that sound so familiar?

❁

"Kurt! Get up off the floor!" I cried, prying Kurt to his feet. He was crawling around the supermarket on his hands and knees, pretending to be a dog.

"Ruff, ruff!" Kurt barked, and fell back to his knees. I picked him up and put him in the grocery cart.

"Now where are your sisters?" I wondered out loud. I heard squealing in another aisle. Brigitta and Louisa must be there. I pushed my cart toward the frozen-foods aisle, following the noise.

Fred appeared with a box of cereal. "Ashley, can we get this? Mom always lets us have it for breakfast."

"No, she doesn't," I said. "She told me you're only allowed to have healthy stuff."

54

"But this *is* healthy!" Fred insisted. "It's fortified with all these vitamins and minerals!"

"Put it back, please," I said firmly.

Brigitta screeched around the corner, chased by Louisa and clutching a bottle of blue-and-green-striped ketchup. She tossed it into the cart without even asking me and ran off again.

"Hey!" I called after her. "We're not buying this!"

The girls ignored me. I loaded the cart with fresh fruits and vegetables and three boxes of organic pasta. Liesl brought a two-liter bottle of soda and dropped it in the cart.

"Liesl—" I began. I was going to say "You're not allowed to have soda." But instead I said, "Oh, never mind. I give up."

There was a thud in the housewares aisle, followed by high-pitched screams. "Come on, Kurt," I said. "That's got to be one of ours."

I sped the cart to the paper-goods section. Kurt pretended we were a firetruck and made siren noises the whole way.

"It's all Louisa's fault!" Brigitta claimed when we got there.

"That's not true!" Louisa cried. "Briggy pushed me!"

A towering display of paper towels had tumbled to the floor. A few of the rolls moved. A skinny guy sat up, blinked, and smiled at me. He looked kind of familiar.

"Are you all right?" I asked.

He stood up. "I'm fine. It takes more than a few rolls of paper towels to hurt me." He bent down to pick up some of the rolls.

"Please, don't do that," I said. "Girls, pick up these paper towels."

A stock boy in a white apron appeared. "I'll do it," he said, and he got to work.

"Ashley, right?" the paper-towel victim said.

"Right," I replied. "And you're . . ."

"Nate," the guy said. "Bill's friend. We rode the ski lift together a couple of days ago."

"Right!" I remembered him now. "Are you sure you're okay?"

"I'm not hurt at all," Nate insisted. "Who are all these children?"

"My friend Nancy is their nanny," I explained. "But she broke her leg yesterday, so I'm helping her out."

"That's very nice of you," Nate said.

"Well, it's not easy," I admitted. "There are five of them, and they're a handful. What are you doing here?"

"I came into town to look around," Nate said. "I stopped in here for a soda, but when I got to the cashier I realized I'd forgotten to bring money!" He

56

laughed a cute kind of snort-laugh. Brigitta, Louisa, and Kurt, who were all listening, laughed, too.

"I can help you finish your grocery shopping," Nate offered. "What else do you need?"

I thought for a minute. "Cheddar cheese, whole-wheat bread, some natural peanut butter."

"We'll get those for you," Nate said, taking Louisa and Brigitta by the hand. "What are your names?" he asked them as they headed for the bread aisle.

"Did you see that, Kurt?" I asked.

"I want to go with them!" Kurt cried.

"You stay here with me," I said.

Nate soon returned with more groceries and Fred and Liesl as well as the little girls. We headed for the checkout line.

"Fred picked out these funny-looking sausages," Nate said, holding up a package of hot dogs.

"Fred," I scolded, "your mother will never let those in the house!"

"But if we eat them all up she'll never know!" Nate said.

The kids laughed.

"I guess I'm outnumbered," I said, tossing the hot dogs onto the checkout counter. "I know when I'm beaten."

I paid for the groceries and a soda for Nate with money the Johansens had left me.

"Want a lift back to Snowbeam?" I asked Nate.

"Yes! Yes!" Brigitta and Louisa jumped up and down and squealed.

"Thanks, that would be great," Nate said.

We piled into the Johansens' huge SUV. I strapped Kurt and Louisa into their car seats. Nate sat up front with me.

Brigitta poked her face between Nate's and mine. "Look what Nate showed me!" she said. She rolled her eyes back in her head, pushed her nose back like a pig's snout, and stuck out her tongue.

"That's beautiful," I said. "Now sit down and buckle your seat belt."

"Ruff, ruff!" Kurt barked.

"Aaoooo!" Nate howled back.

Everyone laughed. Nate had been so shy when I'd first met him that I'd hardly noticed him. But he opened up around the kids. "You're so great with them," I said when we dropped him off at the main lodge. "Especially the little girls."

"They remind me of my sisters," Nate said. "They get bratty if you don't pay enough attention to them."

"Bratty to the extreme," I said, thinking of the mess that waited for me back at the house. A charred pan full of burned noodles, Soupy's muddy footprints . . .

❀

"Hi, Ashley." Mom greeted me with a plate of cheese and crackers when I got home that evening. "Want a little snack before dinner?"

"No, thanks," I said, trudging upstairs to my room. "Must lie down."

"Will you be gracing us with your presence at dinner tonight?" Dad called up the stairs.

"If I don't fall asleep!" I called back.

"How were the Johansens?" Mary-Kate asked, coming into my room.

"Exhausting," I replied. I collapsed on my bed and told her all about it.

"Well, you're just getting to know them," Mary-Kate said. "Maybe it will be easier the next time you baby-sit."

"I hope so," I said. "How was your date?"

"Wonderful!" she cried. She collapsed on the bed beside me. There was a difference, though. I collapsed out of exhaustion, and she collapsed out of happiness.

"It was a perfect day for horseback riding, sunny and not too cold," she reported. "And we stopped at this sweet little inn for lunch. We didn't talk a lot while we were riding, but it was nice. Like we didn't have to talk, you know? But when we stopped to eat, we talked easily." She sighed and kicked her feet into the air. "I really like him."

"Where's he from?" I asked.

"I'm not sure," she said. "Somewhere on the East Coast."

"I thought you said you talked a lot," I teased.

"We did," she insisted. "Just not about that."

"Did you find out anything about him? Where does he go to school?"

"I didn't ask," she said.

I laughed and shook my head. "I can't believe you! I would have grilled him on every detail."

"I know. I'll find out all that stuff eventually, I guess," she said. She sat up. "I did see a clue in his wallet, though. He had an ID from Northrup Academy."

I shot up. "Northrup Academy! Are you kidding me? That's where Prince Stephen goes!"

"It is?" Mary-Kate said. "I thought it sounded familiar. But I didn't make the connection."

"You're a terrible prince-hunter," I said.

Mary-Kate looked thoughtful. "Wow," she said. "Maybe Bill knows the prince!"

"Yeah," I said. "Maybe he knows him. Or maybe he *is* the prince!"

chapter seven

"Bill? The prince?" Mary-Kate laughed. "No way."

"Why not?" I said. "How do you know he's not the prince? The prince is hiding his identity. Maybe Bill's name isn't really Bill. Maybe it's Stephen!"

Mary-Kate shook her head. "I don't think so," she said. "It doesn't feel right. And I don't think he'd lie to me."

"It's not as if he's lying, exactly," I said. "It's to protect himself."

"I'm sure Bill isn't the prince," Mary-Kate said. "I just know. Anyway, we don't have any proof."

"A Northrup ID isn't much to go on, I guess," I admitted. "I mean, there could be a whole group of Northrup guys here for all we know."

I pictured Bill in my mind, trying to remember what he looked like. He was handsome, tall, blond, blue-eyed, broad-shouldered . . . and now, in my imagination, he had a princely glow about him. Like a halo, only less angelic.

"Wouldn't it be fun if it turned out Bill *was* the prince?" I said. "You'd be dating royalty!"

"I don't even want to think about it," Mary-Kate said. "Because he's *not*."

Maybe he is, and maybe he isn't, I thought. *But one way or another, I'm going to find out.*

"Snowbeam reservation desk," a man's voice said. "Michael speaking. May I help you?"

"Hello," I said. "I'd like to make a reservation please. And I'd like the finest accommodations you have. Money is no object."

If I could find out where the prince was staying in the resort, I might be able to track him down. I figured he must have the fanciest digs in the place, right? I mean, come on. He's a prince.

"May I have your name, please?" the man asked.

"Ashley," I replied without thinking. "Uh, Ashley von Rickenbacker."

"What is your date of arrival, Ms. von Rickenbacker?" Michael asked.

"Um . . . next week," I said. "Next Tuesday."

"I'm afraid we're completely booked up next week," Michael said.

"Okay, well . . . how about January? The second week in January."

"All right, I'll check." I could hear Michael tapping on a computer keyboard. "You're in luck. The Presidential Suite is available that week."

"Is that the absolute best place to stay?"

"Yes, Ms. von Rickenbacker," he replied. "It's a full-service suite in the penthouse of the main lodge. Complete privacy and full security. Can I book you for that week?"

"Um, I'll have to think about it," I said. "Thank you!"

That was easy, I thought, hanging up the phone. *Why didn't I think of it before?*

The penthouse. Privacy, security, and full service. I didn't even know the main lodge *had* a penthouse. That's how private it was.

Now we were getting somewhere.

"I am the best! I am so great!" Louisa sang the next morning, banging a pot with a wooden spoon as she paraded through the house. "Give me some candy! Because I'm the best! Or I will kick Briggy in the butt!" *Bang! Bang! Bang!*

"Louisa, stop banging that pot," I warned. I snatched the wooden spoon away from her.

I thought I was going to have the day off. I'd planned to check out the presidential suite and then go skiing. But Mrs. Johansen had called first thing in the morning and begged me to come watch the kids for a while. She and Mr. Johansen had an extra training session.

"Let's go skiing, Ashley," Liesl begged. "It's so nice out! I don't want to stay cooped up in here all day with these little brats."

"Liesl, it's like you're reading my mind," I said. The kids could burn up some of their energy on the slopes. I wanted to find out more about Prince Stephen—and Bill, if that was his real name. But I was saddled with the kids. So I'd just have to do my investigating on the slopes. At least it was better than being stuck in the house.

It took forever to get the kids all bundled up. Finally, when they were ready, we loaded up the SUV and drove to the ski school. Fred and Liesl went off to take a lesson while I stayed on the bunny slope with the little kids.

I was bored. I wished I could snoop around the lodge a little or at least hit the real slopes.

I wondered how Mary-Kate was doing. She was spending the day skiing with Bill. Maybe he'd tell her that he was the prince!

Brigitta and Louisa whizzed down the gentle hill over and over again. I stayed with Kurt, helping him get on and off the lift. The lift lines were crowded with instructors giving lessons to beginners.

"You know my friend Will?" a guy behind me said.

"The room-service waiter?" a girl answered.

I glanced back and saw by their bright blue jackets that they were instructors. I waited to hear more, since I had nothing better to do. Kurt was speaking only in barks that morning.

"Yeah, what about him?" the girl said.

"He delivers room service to the prince," the guy said. "Every night."

My ears perked up. Maybe being stuck on the bunny slope wasn't so bad after all.

"He does?" the girl said. "Has he seen the prince?"

"No," the guy said. "They told him to leave the tray in the foyer of the suite. He never saw anybody."

"Then how does he know it's the prince's room?" the girl asked.

"Because the prince left him a tip in an envelope once, and it had the royal seal of Montavan on it!" the guy explained.

"Wow," the girl said. "Is he a good tipper?"

"I guess," the guy said. "But you know what he eats? A ham-and-cheese sandwich with pickles on it and a banana milkshake. Every night. The same thing. It's like his late-night snack or something."

Aha! I thought. *A clue!*

"That's weird," the girl said. "I mean, pickles? And a banana milkshake? Somehow I thought a prince would eat caviar or duck or something."

65

Kurt and I reached the front of the line. I helped him onto the lift. As we rode up the hill, I heard the girl say, "I wish Will could get to see him. I'm dying to know what he looks like."

Aren't we all, I thought. *But I'll find out, sooner or later.* And if I had my way, it was going to be sooner.

❋

"Check it out, Mary-Kate!" Bill stopped partway down the hill and pointed to a sign. "A race course! Want to try it?"

"Sure," I said. We followed the sign to a real, official ski racetrack. It had a digital timer as big as a billboard, an electronic starting gate and finish line, and flagged obstacles to ski around, just like at the Olympics. It cost a dollar per racer.

"Why don't we make this interesting?" I suggested. "The loser buys lunch."

"You're on," Bill agreed. We lined up at the starting gate and each paid our dollar. "Ladies first," he said.

"That's very old-fashioned," I protested. "Let's flip to see who goes first."

Bill took a quarter from his pocket and tossed it into the air. "Your call."

"Heads."

He caught the coin. "Tails. Too bad. Looks like you're going to have to try to beat my time."

"No problem," I bluffed. Bill was very fast, and I knew it wouldn't be easy to beat him.

He loaded into the starting gate. The buzzer sounded, and he was off. He got a good start, crouched low, and flew past the first few flags. He cut a little too close to the next flag, running over it. That slowed him down a little, but not much. He crossed the finish line in ninety-seven seconds.

"*Woo hoo!*" he called up to me, waving his ski poles in triumph. "Looks like lunch is on you, Olsen!"

"We'll just see about that," I said. I settled into the starting gate. The buzzer sounded. I pushed off as hard as I could and sped down the hill, dodging the flags. If I wanted to beat him, I couldn't hold back. I couldn't play it safe. So I cleared my mind and let my skis do the work. I crossed the finish line and looked at the board. Ninety-four seconds! I'd won!

"Nice run, Olsen," Bill said. "Very impressive. I don't mind buying lunch for a girl who can ski like that, not at all."

"Thank you," I said. "I was in the zone."

"Well, I want a rematch," Bill teased. "And next time you're going first."

A guy stopped us at a little shack at the end of the course. "The winner gets a medal," he said, handing me a cheap, gold-colored pin on a blue ribbon with a picture of a skier and WINNER printed on it.

"Winning gives me an appetite," I said, tucking the medal in my pocket. "I'm ready for that lunch you owe me."

"Me too," Bill said. "Winning gives me an appetite—and so does losing. And so does not racing at all!"

We skied to the nearest café. It was late in the day and they were getting ready to close. We took off our skis and hurried inside.

"You just made it," a woman behind the counter said. "No more hamburgers or hot dogs. All we have left is what's in the sandwich bin."

Bill rummaged through the bin and pulled out two ham-and-cheese sandwiches. "All right with you?" he asked, showing them to me. "The only other choice is egg salad."

"Fine," I said. I sat at a table while he got our drinks and paid for our lunch. Then he brought the food over to me.

"I got the last brownie," he said, sitting down, "to celebrate your surprise victory."

"Surprise?" I said, pretending to be offended. "I was the odds-on favorite."

We unwrapped our sandwiches and started eating. "Let me see that medal," Bill said. I pulled it out of my pocket and handed it to him.

"You should wear this," he said, "so everyone knows you're the champ." He reached over and pinned it on my jacket.

I grinned. He sat back and admired the medal. "I've got to get a picture of that," he said. "Have you got a camera with you?"

I shook my head.

"I've got one in my room," he said. "Let's stop and get the camera after lunch so we can take some pictures this afternoon."

"Cool," I agreed.

We finished the brownie and skied back to the main lodge. "I'll be right back," Bill said, taking off his skis.

"I'll come with you," I offered. I was curious to see his room.

"No, wait here," he said. "It'll just be a minute. Besides, my room is a wreck and I don't want to scare you away."

He returned a few minutes later with the camera. "Let's get a shot of you holding the medal," he said. I unpinned it from my jacket, held it up, and kissed it. *Click*.

Bill laughed. "Great shot. Way to rub it in."

We hit the slopes again for one last run before the sun set. Bill snapped pictures of me posing in front of beautiful views. We even stopped a ski patrol woman and asked her to take a few of the two of us.

"Got any plans for tonight?" he asked as we took off our skis at the end of the day. "A bunch of people are going caroling around the resort. Want to come?"

"Sounds good," I said.

"Bring your sister, too," he added.

"I will," I promised. "If she's not too tired from baby-sitting."

We parted at the lobby. "See you tonight," he said. He leaned down and gave me a little kiss. It was just a peck—but it was on the lips.

Wow, I thought, melting. *I haven't felt this way about a guy in a long time. I forgot how nice it is!*

❀

"He kissed you?" I cried. It was early that evening, and Mary-Kate and I were getting ready to go out caroling. We traded reports on how our days had gone. I had to admit hers sounded more fun than mine. A lot more fun.

"It wasn't a real kiss, exactly," she said. "Very quick."

"Still," I said. "On the lips? It's like he's already your boyfriend."

"It kind of feels that way," Mary-Kate said. "It's very easy between us."

"What else did you do?" I asked.

"We raced, and I beat him, so he bought me lunch."

Aha! Lunch. I remembered what I'd over-heard that day about the prince's midnight snack. "What did he have?" I asked.

"Ham-and-cheese," she answered.

The hair prickled on the back of my neck. "Ham-and-cheese!" I cried. "Do you know what I heard today? Prince Stephen orders a ham-and-cheese sandwich from room service every single night!"

"He does?" Mary-Kate asked.

"Yes," I added. "With pickles and a banana milkshake."

Mary-Kate made a face. "Something about pickles and bananas just doesn't go together."

"I know," I agreed. "But do you see what I'm thinking here? The prince eats ham-and-cheese. Bill eats ham-and-cheese. . . . Get it?"

"Ashley, I had ham-and-cheese for lunch, too," she said. "Does that make me the Prince of Montavan?"

"Obviously *you* couldn't be the prince," I admitted. "You're a girl."

"The only other choice was egg salad, okay?" Mary-Kate said. "Give it up."

"I admit it's kind of weak evidence," I said. "Okay, tell me what else you did today."

"Well, Bill wanted to take a picture of me with my medal, so he went to his room to get his camera, and—"

"He went to his room?" I cried. "Did you see it? Where was it?"

"He didn't want me to go up there," she said. "It was in the main lodge."

I frowned. She just didn't get it! "There are hundreds of rooms in the main lodge," I said. "Where exactly? Did you see what floor he went to? The penthouse, maybe?"

She shrugged. "I didn't notice."

"But he wouldn't let you go up there?" I pressed. "Don't you see? He's hiding something from you!"

"Oh, please." She waved this away. "He's just a slob who doesn't want me to see his messy room."

"I think he didn't want you to see that he's staying in the presidential suite—because he's the prince!" I insisted.

"Ashley, I really don't think he's the prince," Mary-Kate said.

Well, I think he is, and I'm going to find out once and for all, I vowed. *The first chance I get, I'm going to go up to that Presidential Suite. I'm going to knock on the door—and see who answers!*

72

chapter eight

"This is Carina, Jack, Adam, and Suzanne," Bill said later that night. We had gathered in the lobby of the main lodge to meet everyone and go caroling.

"You've met Nate," he added, to Carina and her friends. "And this is Ashley and Mary-Kate." He put his arm around Mary-Kate.

Carina, Jack, Adam, and Suzanne smiled and nodded at us.

"I downloaded some carols off the Internet," Suzanne said, handing us each a few sheets of paper. "In case some of us don't know all the words."

"Thanks," I said. She'd printed up the lyrics to a dozen traditional Christmas songs. "That was a good idea."

"Where should we start?" Bill asked. He was dressed in jeans, a blue sweater, a red scarf, and a very nice brown leather jacket, unzipped.

"Check it out," Adam said, flipping open Bill's jacket. Inside it was lined with blue-and-green-striped fabric. "Whoa, silk lining!"

"Okay, okay," Bill said good-naturedly, snapping his jacket closed. "Fashion show's over. You want me to bring up the fur hat you were wearing the other night, Adam?"

Adam grinned. "Hey, man, all I'm saying is you look cool."

"We'd better get started or a lot of the littler kids will be in bed," Suzanne said. "I think we should hit the townhouses first."

We left the lobby and walked through the narrow, snowy streets toward the townhouses. Bill took Mary-Kate's hand. I walked next to Nate. He seemed shy again now that there were so many people around.

"Do you all know 'Good King Wenceslas'?" Suzanne asked. She started singing the song, and we all joined in.

"Hey—isn't this our house?" Mary-Kate asked as we approached a row of townhouses.

Mom and Dad opened the front door and stepped out. "Hello, girls!" Mom waved.

"Hi, Mom and Dad." We introduced them to everyone. "Any requests?"

"Let me guess," Mary-Kate said. "You want 'I Saw Mommy Kissing Santa Claus.' Right?"

It was Dad's favorite Christmas song. So embarrassing.

"Well, I was going to request 'All I Want for Christmas Is My Two Front Teeth,'" Dad said. "But if you insist—"

We sang the embarrassing song. Mom and Dad thanked us and offered us some snacks. Then it was time to move on.

"Good to see you, girls!" Dad joked. "Come back anytime!"

"Your parents are cool," Bill said.

We wound our way through the townhouse section, stopping on each block to sing. Finally we found our way back to the main lodge.

"Let's go from floor to floor," I suggested. My secret plan was to hit every floor in the lodge—including the penthouse. "These people are carol-deprived!"

"I don't know," Bill said. "I'm hungry."

"Me too," Jack added. "And I'm kind of tired of singing."

"No! Come on!" I protested. "We'll just whip through the lodge, starting at the top floor. It won't take long."

"I think I'm ready to quit," Adam said.

"Let's go get something to eat," Carina said.

They headed for some seats by the fireplace. A waitress took our orders and disappeared.

Okay, so my plan didn't work. I was still set on finding a way to get up to that penthouse.

"So who's going to the party?" Carina asked as we settled near the fire.

"I'm going," Adam said. "My mother's making me wear a tuxedo."

"What party?" Jack asked. But I knew exactly what party he was talking about—the big, exclusive Christmas Eve party.

"Were you invited?" I asked Carina.

She nodded. I recognized her last name—Molinari—and figured her father was probably the famous Hollywood producer, Frank Molinari.

"I wish I could go," Suzanne said. "I heard it's amazing. All the celebrities go. And Cargo is playing at the party!" Cargo is a popular rock band.

"Wow—I didn't know that!" I said. Christmas Eve was only four days away and I still hadn't found a way to go to the party.

"You're not invited?" Carina asked.

"No," I said. I glanced at Bill, who hadn't said anything. "Were you invited?" I asked him.

Bill said, "No, I wasn't invited."

Mary-Kate flashed me a look that said, "See. I told you he's not the prince!" But I wasn't convinced. If he was lying about his name to hide his identity, he could lie about other things, too. Maybe he *was* invited, but he didn't want us to know.

"How are the kids doing?" Nate asked me.

"They're fine," I said. "*I'm* the one who's about to have a nervous breakdown."

Nate laughed. "I thought of something that might keep them busy. You could teach the kids a few Christmas carols and put on a concert for their parents."

"Nate, that's a great idea!" I said. "It could be just like *The Sound of Music*, where the governess teaches the kids to sing. The Johansens are really into that movie, you know."

"I thought all those Austrian names sounded familiar," Nate said.

"I don't know if I could handle it by myself, though," I added. "How will I get all five kids to sit still in one room at the same time? It's impossible!"

The waitress returned with our hot chocolate and snacks. Everyone reached into their pockets to pay for their own food. Nate patted his pants pocket, then his coat pocket. He pulled out a dollar and some change. Not enough to pay for his cocoa and soup.

Bill leaned over and said quietly to Nate, "Don't worry, I've got you covered."

It was the second time I'd seen Nate caught without enough cash. *He must need some extra money*, I thought. *Poor guy*.

"Nate, I've got an idea," I said. "Why don't you help me with the kids' Christmas concert? They

77

love you, and I could use the help. I'll pay you half my salary." Then he'd have pocket money to spend.

"Sounds fun," Nate said. "I'd love to do it."

"Great!" I said. "When can you start? We don't have much time."

"How about tomorrow?" Nate said.

I was supposed to baby-sit the next day. Maybe having Nate there would make it easier.

"Tomorrow is perfect," I said.

"Ashley, I want to go out and play," Louisa whined. "Why can't I go skiing today?"

"Because you have a cold," I said. "So we all have to stay in." *Even though it's the most gorgeous day yet*, I thought.

I sat on Louisa's bed with her, watching a video. The other kids were downstairs in the kitchen making Christmas ornaments out of colored paper and glitter.

"Ruff, ruff!" Kurt crawled in on his hands and knees, pretending to be Soupy again. He crawled right up to Louisa and—*chomp!*—bit her on the ankle!

"*Ow!*" Louisa shrieked.

"Kurt, what did you do that for?" I asked.

"I'm a doggy," Kurt said, his tongue hanging out of his mouth.

"Punish him!" Louisa demanded.

"Let me see your ankle," I said. There were little red teeth marks, but he hadn't broken the skin. "You'll be all right," I told Louisa. "I'll get some ice for it."

I dragged Kurt downstairs with me. "Kurt, you're not a dog, you're a boy," I said for the hundredth time. "And even if you were a dog, you should never bite anyone! Soupy doesn't bite, does he?"

Kurt stared blankly at me and barked again.

I got ice for Louisa's ankle, and the doorbell rang. I peered through the window and smiled. Nate! I opened the door.

"I'm so glad to see you," I said.

"I'm glad to see you, too," Nate replied. "Ready for some singing?"

"I don't know," I said. "I haven't mentioned your idea to the kids yet. I don't know how they'll take it."

"They'll love it," Nate said. "Come on." He stepped into the kitchen. "Hey, kids, what are you doing?"

"Nate!" Liesl cried. She, Fred, and Brigitta jumped up from their chairs to say hello. Kurt wrapped his little body around Nate's leg and wouldn't let go.

"Who's down there?" Louisa called from upstairs.

"Hi, Louisa!" Nate called back.

"Nate!" she cried, and ran downstairs.

"Listen," Nate said. "I've got a special project for you kids. I want to know what you think of it."

"What is it?" Liesl asked.

"How would you like to surprise your parents with a Christmas concert?" Nate said. "Ashley and I will teach you some carols. We could do it the day before Christmas Eve, after the triathlon. What do you think?"

"Yay!" the kids cried.

"Good," Nate said. "We've got a lot of work to do. The concert is only two days away."

He herded them into the living room and lined them up by height. "Which song should we start with?" he asked me.

"How about 'Edelweiss'?" I said. "Everybody knows that."

He led the kids in a chorus of "Edelweiss." They sang at the top of their lungs. The only problem was, they were terrible! Every single one of them! Worst of all, Kurt barked his way through almost every song.

I glanced over at Nate. He shrugged and whispered, "I'm sure their parents won't mind, right?"

"Anybody home?" Mr. Johansen called. He and Mrs. Johansen walked in.

"You're home early," I said. I introduced them to Nate.

"We finished up early at practice today," Mrs. J. said. "I thought we'd come home and give you and Nate the afternoon off."

"Great!" I said. "Thank you."

Nate and I left, promising the kids we'd see them bright and early the next morning.

"What should we do with our afternoon off?" I asked Nate.

"Why don't we hit the slopes?" Nate suggested. "We can meet up with Bill and Mary-Kate and everybody." Mary-Kate and Bill were skiing with Carina, Suzanne, and Jack.

"Sounds good," I agreed. "I'll go change and get my skis. I'll meet you at the lift-ticket booth."

"Deal."

Half an hour later I found Nate waiting for me at the ticket booth. We bought our lift-tickets and headed for the slopes to meet Mary-Kate and the others.

"Nate! Come on!" I called. "I see Mary-Kate and Bill!"

We put on our skis and joined Mary-Kate and Bill in the lift line.

"The snow is excellent today," Bill told us. "Some fresh powder fell early this morning."

We rode up the lift in two groups. At the top

of the mountain, we discussed which run to take.

"I can't do black diamonds," Suzanne said. "I only learned how to ski last year."

"Come on, Suze," Jack teased. "You can do it. I'll help you." He playfully tossed a handful of snow at her.

"No, I can't," Suzanne insisted. She picked up some snow, packed it tight, and threw it at him. It hit him in the leg.

"Oh, so you're looking for a snowball fight, are you?" Jack said. He bent down to gather some snow.

"Hey—don't start," Carina said. She picked up some snow and stuffed it down Jack's jacket.

Jack stood up, red-faced. "Ooh, you're asking for it now, Carina," he said. He threw his snowball at her. Carina threw one back, and Suzanne nailed him with one, too.

"You want in on this action?" Bill asked Mary-Kate.

"Too late!" Mary-Kate shouted. She lobbed a snowball at his chest. "I'm already in!"

Nate and I joined in. At first everyone played kind of lightly, but soon it got rowdy. Carina pushed Jack down in the snow. Suzanne dumped a whole armful of snow on Bill's head. One of my shots missed and hit an innocent skier passing by.

"What's going on here?" a voice shouted. Two ski patrol guys skied up to us and stopped. Just as they arrived, Suzanne aimed a snowball at me. She tried to stop her arm, but the momentum was too strong. The snowball flew through the air, missed me, and hit a ski patrol guy right in the middle of his yellow jacket.

Uh-oh.

The ski patrol guy frowned. "That wasn't very smart," he said. "Snowball fights are forbidden on the slopes. You'll all have to come with us."

I glanced at Mary-Kate. Oh, no. Were we in trouble?

chapter nine

"**R**oughhousing on skis can be very dangerous," the ski patrol guy said.

"We're sorry," I said. "We didn't mean for it to get out of hand."

"You could get into serious trouble," the ski patrol guy said. "If anyone endangers our guests, we have the right to keep them off the slopes."

We all gasped. Was he threatening to keep us from skiing?

"Excuse me, sir," Bill said politely, skiing up to the ski patrol guys. "Can I talk to you a minute?"

He pulled one of the ski patrol guys aside and told him something in a low voice. They whispered back and forth for a few minutes. The ski patrol guy nodded and whispered something to his partner. Then he nodded politely at us.

"All right," he said. "We're letting you off with a warning. Please—no more snowball fights. Have a good time, and enjoy your stay at Snowbeam."

They skied away. I watched them, amazed. What had just happened? Why had they suddenly backed off?

What had Bill said to them? I had a hunch.

I skied up to Mary-Kate. "Did you see that?" she whispered. "One minute we're in big trouble, and the next minute he says, `Have a good time!'"

"Isn't it obvious?" I said. "Bill must have told them that he is the prince!"

Mary-Kate stared at me. "Ashley, stop it. That can't be it."

"What else could it be?" I said. "Why else would the ski patrol suddenly back off like that? Did you see the way they practically bowed to him?"

Mary-Kate shook her head. "No. No, that can't be it! I'll admit that it's weird, but it doesn't prove anything. Bill is good at taking charge of things. I've seen him do it. Maybe he has a lot of influence at the resort."

"Yeah," I said. "He has a lot of influence because he's the prince!"

I was completely convinced. There were too many little clues adding up—and all pointing to Bill. Why couldn't Mary-Kate see that?

"Mary-Kate, I am absolutely sure that you are dating the Prince of Montavan."

And I'm going to prove it to you tonight! I thought. *Presidential Suite, here I come!*

"That was a long walk," Mary-Kate said later that night. "Where did you go?"

Mom and Dad were already in bed. Mary-Kate sat curled on the couch in the living room, watching TV.

"I went to get your proof," I told her. "And I got it."

She frowned. "What? You stole a strand of Bill's hair and performed a DNA test on it? You spotted a tattoo on Bill's back that says DEAR ASHLEY, I AM PRINCE STEPHEN?"

Not quite as good as that," I said, "but pretty good. I went to the Presidential Suite to see if Bill would answer the door."

She nodded. "All right. So what happened?"

"The valet was just coming out of the room with a bunch of clothes to be cleaned."

Mary-Kate rolled her eyes. "Great. So what did the valet tell you?"

"Nothing. But he was carrying Bill's brown leather jacket." I grinned victoriously. "The exact same one he was wearing the other night. Remember how Adam teased him about the lining?"

"It was the same?" Mary-Kate asked. "The blue-and-green stripes?"

"The blue-and-green stripes," I said.

"Well, Bill and Prince Stephen could have bought the same jacket," Mary-Kate said.

"But it's a pretty big coincidence, don't you think?" I insisted. "Maybe the jacket alone isn't proof, but put it with everything else and it's obvious! Think about it—he has a Northrup Academy ID, which means he probably goes to the same school as Prince Stephen. He has the same jacket as the prince. He's hiding something. He's mysterious about where he's from. He won't let you see where he's staying. He always has plenty of money and seems to be very well-off. He has this weird power to call off the ski patrol whenever he wants. And don't forget the ham-and-cheese sandwiches."

Mary-Kate frowned at me.

"Okay," I said. "Maybe not the sandwiches. But you can't deny the rest."

Mary-Kate closed her eyes and rested her head against the back of the couch. "Maybe you're right," she admitted. "A lot of things point to him being the prince."

"Finally!" I said. "What took you so long to come over to my side?"

"I don't want Bill to be the prince," she said. "I mean, it's exciting and everything. But I really like him—as a regular guy, not as royalty. I was kind of hoping we could keep in touch after we leave

87

Snowbeam. I know he lives far away, but we could E-mail and visit on vacations. . . ."

"But you could still do that if he's the prince," I said. "What's the difference?"

"Think about it, Ashley. If he's the prince, how could we ever have a normal relationship? He has to hide his identity for security reasons, everyone wants to know about everything he does, and there'd be so much pressure on any girl he dates. Is he going to marry her? Is she good enough to be the Princess of Montavan?"

"But that's so cool!" I cried. "You could be Princess Mary-Kate of Montavan!"

"But I don't want to be Princess Mary-Kate of Montavan," she protested. "I just want to be me. And I want Bill to be Bill." She sighed. "I just really like him."

I sat beside her. "Well, I'm sorry to hear that," I said. "Because I'm pretty sure Bill is not Bill. He's Stephen. So dust off your tiara—you're dating a prince."

"No, Ashley," she said. "I'm still not convinced. Not until you give me absolutely undeniable slap-in-the-face proof."

Ugh! She can be so difficult sometimes!

"Well," I said to Nate the next day after another Johansen Christmas concert rehearsal. "No one will ever confuse them with the Vienna Boys Choir."

The Vienna Boys Choir is famous for singing Christmas songs very, very well. No one in the Vienna Boys Choir barked.

"But I think Mr. and Mrs. J. will like it. And they'll love 'A Very Johansen Christmas.'"

Nate had written a very cute song to the tune of "Holly Jolly Christmas" with special lyrics about all the Johansens.

"We can practice the songs again tomorrow before Mr. and Mrs. J. come home from training," Nate said.

The triathlon was the next day, and we planned to surprise the parents with the concert when they got home, as a kind of double celebration. Then the next night I had to come back and baby-sit while Mr. and Mrs. J. went out to the fabulous Christmas Eve party.

"It's just as well," I said. "I don't have anything special to do on Christmas Eve. Mary-Kate and Mom and Dad are going to wait up and celebrate with me when I get home. But I wish I could go to the party."

"Why?" Nate asked. "I'll bet it's nothing special."

"Are you kidding?" I said. "I peeked into that upstairs ballroom where they're holding the party and saw some of the decorations. It looks like a fairyland. I've never seen anything like it." I sighed. "It just seems like a really special way to celebrate Christmas."

And if I could just go to the party, maybe I could find out for sure who the prince is. I imagined it would be obvious. He'd have the best table at the party, be surrounded by his entourage. . . .

"How well do you know Bill?" I asked Nate. After all, they were together when we met. They seemed to be friends. But I wasn't sure how they knew each other.

"Bill? Um, I don't know. . . ." Nate said. "Why?"

"Do you think he could be Prince Stephen?" I asked. "In disguise, I mean?"

Nate laughed. "Bill? I never thought about it. But who knows? I guess anybody could be the prince."

"I think he is," I confessed. "Remember what happened after our snowball fight on the slopes? Why did the ski patrol drop the whole thing so quickly?"

Nate shrugged.

"And he's kind of mysterious with Mary-Kate—like he's hiding something," I went on. "But Mary-Kate doesn't believe me."

"Maybe he *is* hiding something," Nate said. "That doesn't mean he's the prince."

"I know, I know," I said. I'd heard enough of that kind of talk from Mary-Kate. "Still, even if he's not the prince, he's dating my sister. So I want to know what the big secret is. Maybe you can help me."

"Me?" Nate said. "How?"

"You brought your laptop with you, right?" I said. He'd mentioned it to me once, as I had left mine at home. "I'm going to give you a little assignment—find out everything you can about the Prince of Montavan. And while you're at it, find out whatever you can about Bill—if they're not the same person."

Nate grinned. "Sure. No problem. I'll search on-line tonight."

"Thanks, Nate," I said. The more I got to know Nate, the more I liked him. He was always coming to my rescue.

"We've hardly seen you girls all week," Dad complained at dinner that night. "This is supposed to be a family vacation."

"Sorry, Dad," Mary-Kate said. "It's just that, well, we've made some new friends, and they're keeping us busy."

"And I've been working," I added. "I've hardly had a vacation at all."

"Poor Ashley," Mom said. "I know what it's like, believe me. But it will all be over in a couple of days, right? And then you can relax and celebrate Christmas with us."

I nodded. "The triathlon is tomorrow. So after the Christmas Eve party the next night, I'm free."

"Admit it, you're going to miss those kids," Mary-Kate teased.

"We'll see about that," I said.

The doorbell rang. "I wonder who that could be," Mom said.

I stood up and said, "I'll get it."

I answered the door. A messenger in a Snowbeam Resort uniform said, "Olsen?"

"Yes," I said.

"For you." He handed me an envelope.

"Thank you," I said. I closed the door.

The envelope was large and square and trimmed in gold. On the front was written, "The Olsen Family."

"Who was it?" Dad asked.

"A messenger," I explained. "He gave me this." I showed them the envelope.

"Open it!" Mary-Kate cried.

I tore open the envelope and pulled out a printed card. "'The management of the Snowbeam Resort cordially invites you to their annual Christmas Eve Gala. . . .'"

"Oh wow!" I squealed. "We're invited to the party!"

chapter ten

"**W**ho sent it?" Mary-Kate jumped up and read the invitation over my shoulder.

"I don't know," I said. "It doesn't say."

"Let me see." Mary-Kate snatched the invitation away.

"Why don't you ask the messenger who sent it," Dad suggested.

"Good idea." I hurried to the front door. No messenger.

"Hello!" I called into the darkness. "Messenger! Are you still out there?" I ran down the walk to see if I could spot him down the street. But he was gone.

"Too late," I reported when I came back inside.

Mom studied the envelope. "Who could have sent it?"

I had my theories. "Ask Mary-Kate," I said.

"What? I don't know anything," Mary-Kate protested.

"Come on, Mary-Kate," I said. "It had to be Bill! Who else could it be?"

"Maybe the"—she glanced at the card—"'management of the Snowbeam Resort' just felt that we should be included."

"All of a sudden? At the last minute?" I said. "Why?"

Mary-Kate shrugged. "Well, now that they've met us, maybe they think we're cool."

"Oh, please."

"Anyway, it couldn't be Bill," Mary-Kate added. "He already asked me out for Christmas Eve. We have plans."

"What kind of plans?" I asked.

"I don't know yet," Mary-Kate admitted.

"Maybe he was planning on taking you to the party," I said.

"If that's true, why didn't he just say so?" she said.

I shook my head. "You just don't get it, do you?"

Then a terrible, horrible, absolutely earth-shattering thought came to me.

"Oh, no!" I cried. "I can't go!"

"Oh, that's right," Dad said. "The Johansens are going—"

"—and they're expecting me to baby-sit," I finished. Why did this have to happen to me? All I wanted was to get invited to the Christmas party. And when I'm finally invited, I can't go.

"What about Nate?" Mary-Kate said. "Maybe he can fill in for you."

"I can't do that to Nate," I said. "Do you know what it's going to be like, alone with those five kids on Christmas Eve? They'll be bouncing off the walls. And besides, he might have plans already."

Mom put her arm around my shoulder. "I'm sorry, Ashley. What if we watched the kids for you? Then you could go."

I brightened for a second. But then I realized I couldn't do that to Mom and Dad on Christmas Eve. The Johansens were my responsibility. I had volunteered for it, and I had to finish the job.

"Nate, you'll never guess what happened last night," I said.

"I won't even try to guess, Ashley," Nate said. "What happened?"

I was sitting with Nate in the Johansens' kitchen the next day. It was the day before Christmas Eve— the day of the concert. Louisa's cold was better, and she and Brigitta were upstairs playing in their room. Liesl sat on her bed with her earphones on, wrapping presents. Fred was in the living room playing Christmas music on the stereo and trying to make Kurt dance. Soupy was out in the yard.

Nate and I were fixing a special pre-concert Christmas lunch for the kids: cream-of-broccoli soup (green), Tater Tots with ketchup (red), and grilled cheese sandwiches. Nate had picked up a box of decorated Christmas cookies on his way over.

"You won't believe it. We got an anonymous invitation to the party!" I told him.

"You have no idea who sent it?" Nate asked.

"No idea." I sliced some cheese. "But it doesn't really matter, because I can't go."

"Why—because of them?" Nate said, gesturing vaguely toward the kids. "Don't worry about that, Ashley. I'll fill in for you."

I smiled at him. He was one of the sweetest guys I'd ever met. I didn't know how I could have survived the Johansens without him.

"That's so nice of you, Nate," I said. "But I just can't do that to you. It doesn't seem right."

"I don't mind—really," Nate told her. "You should go to the party. It means so much to you."

"No, I'm used to the idea now," I said, though it wasn't quite true. "Mary-Kate can go with Bill and tell me all about it."

"Speaking of Bill," Nate said, reaching into his backpack. "I did the research you asked for, and I found out a few things."

"Really? What?" I sat down at the kitchen table to hear.

He opened a notebook and read from something he'd scribbled on a page. "Well, I found some articles in the *Montavan Morning News*, the biggest daily newspaper there," he began. "Obviously, some people in Montavan know what the prince looks like, but they were careful to be vague when they talked about him. I did see him referred to as tall and well-built."

My eyebrows shot up. "Bill is tall and well-built," I said.

Nate nodded. "And here's something from a gossip column in London. 'Prince Stephen is in town for Wimbledon this year. He has been seen escorting a different beauty around town every night. A waiter at the exclusive Two-Ten Restaurant reports that the prince complained about his Dover sole and had it sent back to the kitchen four times.'"

"Really?" I said. That didn't sound like Bill at all. Since he'd been at Snowbeam he'd only had eyes for Mary-Kate. And I'd never seen him complain about food or service. But who knew? Maybe the Dover sole at that restaurant was really terrible.

"There was also a report in the *New York Beacon*," Nate went on. "'Prince Stephen of Montavan spent $20,000 at Cartier yesterday. Eyewitnesses report that when the salesperson wasn't quick enough in getting a diamond watch he wanted to see, he snapped at her so fiercely she left the sales floor in tears.'"

My mouth fell open. "What an arrogant jerk!" I exclaimed. "I had no idea the prince was so rude."

"I guess so," Nate said. "That is, if you believe what you read in the papers."

My head was spinning. "I have to admit, this doesn't sound much like the Bill we know, does it?"

"No, it doesn't," Nate agreed.

"Maybe I'm wrong about him," I said. "Maybe he's not the prince. But if he isn't, what is he hiding? And who invited us to the party?"

"Maybe you'll never know," Nate said.

"Never know?" I cried. "Impossible. I can't stand not knowing."

Suddenly, screams came from upstairs. "That sounds like Louisa," Nate said.

We ran upstairs to see what was wrong. Liesl was sitting in her room as if she hadn't heard a thing. Louisa and Brigitta were rolling on the floor clawing and kicking at each other.

Nate pulled them apart. "Girls! What's wrong? This isn't how the sweet little munchkins I know behave."

"Yeah, right," I said. "What's the matter?"

"Louisa pinched me!" Brigitta complained.

"Well, she called me carrot-head!" Louisa said.

"But you are a carrot-head," Brigitta said. "You have red hair."

"So do you, stupid!" Louisa said.

"You're all carrot-heads," I said. "It's not worth getting upset about. When you grow up, you can dye your hair if you want."

"Ashley!" Fred came racing up the stairs and burst into the girls' room. "Kurt is gone!"

"What do you mean?" I asked. "Wasn't he with you?"

"He wouldn't dance for me, so I let him go in the den and watch a video," Fred explained. "He must have gone outside to be with Soupy. But somebody left the back gate open. And now Kurt *and* Soupy are gone!"

"What?" Nate and I raced downstairs and searched every room, trailed by the kids. Then we ran outside. Just as Fred had said, the back gate was open, and there were no Kurt and Soupy.

"Soupy must have wandered through the open gate," Nate said, "and Kurt probably followed him."

We hurried to the front yard, but they weren't there.

"We've got to find them!" I said. I looked all around, wondering where they might go. "I'll check the woods behind the backyard. Brigitta and Louisa, you come with me. I don't want anyone else to get lost."

"We'll search all the neighbors' yards," Liesl said, nodding at Fred.

"I'll follow the road down to the ski center," Nate said. "They might have wandered down there."

"Okay, let's go," I said. "Everybody be careful."

I took the two little girls by the hand and headed for the woods. *Please let us find them soon*, I prayed. *Or it won't be a very merry Christmas for anyone.*

❀

"What about this little purse?" Bill asked me. "Would Ashley like that?"

I picked up the small silver bag. "It's beautiful," I said. "But she already has one almost exactly like it."

Bill and I had gone into town to do some last-minute Christmas shopping. So far I had found something for everyone on my list except Ashley. Usually she was the easiest to shop for—I knew her taste cold. I couldn't understand why I was having trouble with her this year.

"I didn't realize you girls were so picky," Bill teased. "I hope you'll like what I got for you. Or maybe you already have something like it!"

"I'm sure I'll love it," I said. I couldn't wait to see

what Bill had gotten me for Christmas. We'd only met a few days earlier, but it felt as if I'd known him forever. Still, I had trouble when I was shopping for him. What if he was Prince Stephen? He probably had everything he could ever want. I brushed that thought out of my mind. Ashley was getting to me. But I knew Bill wasn't the prince. In spite of all Ashley's evidence, I still wasn't convinced.

Anyway, I finally did find a present that was just right for him: a blue-and-green-striped scarf to match the lining of his leather jacket.

We strolled hand in hand through the cute little town. The snowy street was lined with small wooden buildings from the 1800s, now occupied by arty boutiques and galleries. The streets bustled with shoppers and carolers and Santas ringing bells. When it came to feeling Christmasy, Snowbeam beat Malibu by a mile.

"Let's stop and have some lunch," I suggested when we came to a diner. "Maybe I'll get a brilliant idea after we eat."

"Good idea," Bill agreed. We went in and sat at the counter.

"I'll have tuna salad on rye toast and a diet soda," I ordered after studying the menu.

Bill never even glanced at it. "I'd like ham and cheese on white with pickles on it," he ordered. "And a banana milkshake."

My heart stopped cold. I wasn't sure I'd heard him right.

"What did you just order?" I asked him.

"Ham-and-cheese with pickles," he replied. "And a banana milkshake. Why, don't you approve?"

"No, it's not that." My mind was racing. I couldn't deny it any longer. It couldn't be a coincidence. I'd never heard of anyone in my life ordering that combination before.

Bill had to be the prince.

What should I do? What should I do? I thought nervously. Bill was keeping a secret from me, and now I was keeping one from him—that I knew his secret. *I'm just going to come right out and ask him for the truth*, I decided.

The waitress set our drinks down on the counter. When she left, I leaned close to Bill and whispered, "Bill, is that your real name?"

He looked surprised and pulled away from me slightly. "Why would you ask me something like that?"

I took a deep breath. "Ashley thinks you're Prince Stephen," I explained.

His eyes widened. "She does?"

I nodded. "She overheard someone saying that the prince orders a ham-and-cheese sandwich with pickles and a banana milkshake every

102

night. And now you just ordered exactly the same thing. . . ."

He turned his head and stared down at the counter.

"And there were other things, too," I went on. "Like how the ski patrol let us go after you talked to them. . . ." I went through Ashley's list of evidence, feeling a little embarrassed. "And finally, someone sent us an anonymous invitation to the Christmas Eve party," I finished. "We thought it might have been you."

Bill gripped the edge of the counter, still staring at it. He looked upset. I was beginning to regret saying anything.

"I'm sorry, Bill," I said. "I didn't mean to upset you. . . ."

At last he turned to face me. "It's okay, Mary-Kate," he said quietly. "I'm not upset. It's time I was straight with you.

"The answer is yes. I am Prince Stephen of Montavan."

chapter eleven

I was stunned. Bill was the prince!

I knew it was possible. But to hear him come right out and say it like that . . . I could hardly breathe.

"Are you okay?" he said. "It's not a big deal, really."

I caught my breath. "Not a big deal? Are you kidding me?"

"No, I'm not kidding," he said. "Why should it change anything between us?"

I shook my head. Maybe he was right. What was the big deal?

But then I looked at him, and suddenly he seemed different. All glossy and shiny and untouchable. And I felt a huge gulf open up between us.

I was dating a prince! It was awesome in a way. But deep down, I knew it meant our relationship was doomed.

Still, if he didn't want to see it that way, I was willing to play along.

"I guess it shouldn't change anything," I said. "Let's just have a happy Christmas together."

"One thing, Mary-Kate," he said. "*Please* keep my identity a secret. I'm trying to keep a low profile while I'm here. . . . Believe me, it's better this way. You can tell Ashley if you want to. But no one else."

"I promise," I said.

"So now that Ashley will know the truth, she can relax and stop investigating, right?" he added.

"I'm sure she'll be glad to hear she was right all along," I said. "But, Bill—I mean—What should I call you? Should I call you Stephen now? I mean, when other people aren't around."

"Keep calling me Bill," he said. "I like the way you say it. And it's the name I'm using while I'm here."

"That's easy enough," I said.

But the rest of the afternoon wasn't so easy. "Bill" and I—I really didn't know what to call him in my own mind—finished our lunch and our shopping. He helped me pick out a very cool necklace for Ashley. But the whole time I felt as if I was watching him from afar. A voice in my head kept squawking, "He's the prince! He's the prince!" Everything he did seemed different now. If he picked up a ski magazine, I thought, *So Prince Stephen reads* Ski

Monthly . . . *interesting*. It's hard to explain, but all of a sudden Bill seemed to belong to everybody all around us. He wasn't just mine anymore.

And I felt sad about it. Because I really liked him.

❀

"Any sign of them?" I asked.

Liesl shook her head. "We checked every yard. Nobody's seen them."

Louisa, Brigitta, and I were returning from searching the woods for Kurt and Soupy. Fred and Liesl were waiting for us at home. Nate was still out searching somewhere.

Louisa clutched my hand and started to cry. "Ashley, what are we going to do? I want Kurt and Soupy to come home."

I stroked her red hair. "So do I," I said. I glanced at the clock. Kurt had been missing for an hour already. Where could they have gone? What if something terrible had happened to them?

What if we never found them?

I picked up the phone. There was only one thing left to do. I had to call the police and report Kurt missing.

Please come home, Kurt, I thought. *And please be okay.*

chapter twelve

I picked up the phone. Then I heard barking in the distance. "What was that?" I said. I stopped, holding the phone poised to my ear.

A dog barked again, from somewhere down the street. But it was coming closer.

I hung up the phone. The kids and I ran out the front door and looked down the street.

Soupy! He barked happily at the sight of us. Leading him down the street was Nate, carrying Kurt on his shoulders.

"Kurt!" I shouted. We ran toward them. I lifted Kurt from Nate's shoulders and hugged him tight. Louisa and Brigitta threw their arms around Soupy.

"Are they all right?" I asked Nate. "Where did you find them?"

"They're fine," Nate said. "I found them all the way down the hill, near the rescue dogs' kennel."

"The kennel!" I cried. "Kurt, what were you doing there?"

Kurt barked at me. I frowned and said, "Come on, Kurt. Answer me in people talk."

"I followed Soupy," Kurt said. "He wanted to see the other doggies."

I turned to Nate. "But how did you know?"

"I had a feeling Soupy might be drawn down there," Nate said. "A ski patrol girl told me that sometimes other dogs from the area turn up at the kennel. Dogs are pack animals. They like to be with other dogs."

"Nate, you're a genius!" I threw my arms around him and kissed him on the cheek. "Thank you, thank you, thank you!"

The other children swarmed around him and hugged him, too. "You're a hero!" Liesl cried. Nate laughed.

"Hey, it was nothing," he said. "But listen—your folks are going to be home soon. And we have a Christmas concert to put on!"

We all hurried back inside the house for a quick rehearsal. I was so happy and relieved, even the kids' singing sounded good to my ears.

Just before dinnertime, Mr. and Mrs. J. came home. Mrs. J. was beaming and she carried a silver trophy.

"Kids, your old mom did it again!" Mr. J.

shouted proudly. "The women's triathlon champ two years in a row!"

"Hurray!" the kids shouted, gathering around their parents.

"Your dad didn't do so badly either," Mrs. J. said. "He came in third."

Mr. J. flashed a bronze medal. "Last year I was fifth," he said, "so I'm doing better."

"Congratulations!" I said. "Sit down here in the living room and relax. The kids have a surprise for you."

I got hot drinks for Mr. and Mrs. J. while they settled on the couch. Nate lined up the kids. Then he turned to his audience.

"The Johansen Children present a special Christmas Concert just for you," Nate announced. Then he led the kids in their first carol, "Away in a Manger."

The kids screeched and squawked their way through the songs. They really were terrible singers. But Mr. and Mrs. J. had tears in their eyes. When the concert was over, they gave the kids a standing ovation.

"Bravo! Bravo!" Mr. J. shouted. He and his wife hugged each of the kids proudly.

"That was beautiful," Mrs. J. said, wiping away a tear. "The best Christmas present I've ever gotten."

I smiled. *A parent's love for a child must be a pretty powerful thing*, I thought, *if it can overcome that singing*.

"Ashley and Nate, thank you so much for all you've done," Mrs. J. said. "I can't tell you how much we appreciate your help after Nancy broke her leg." She picked up her trophy and added, "I never could have gotten this without you."

"The kids are crazy about you," Mr. J. said. "And this concert was just above and beyond. You two are really special."

I glanced at Nate, who was blushing. "Thank you," I said. "We enjoyed it."

And when I looked back on it, I realized that I really did have fun with those kids—chaos, crises, and all.

"I know we asked you to baby-sit tomorrow night," Mrs. J. continued, "but we'd like to give you the night off. You deserve it. And we want to spend Christmas Eve with the children this year."

"Thank you!" I said. Now I could go to the Christmas Eve party! Everything was working out great!

Mr. J. paid Nate and me for our work. We said good-bye to the kids—I knew I'd be seeing a lot more of them, since they were right next door—and left.

Nate grinned at me. "That's lucky. Now you can go to the party."

"I know," I replied. "And I have a favor to ask you."

"I'm up for anything," he said. I grinned, because it was so true. He was a great friend.

"Will you come to the party with me tomorrow night?" I asked. "As my guest? Christmas Eve just wouldn't feel right without you."

"I can't think of anyone I'd rather be with on Christmas Eve," he said. "I'll pick you up at seven."

"Excellent," I said. We stopped in front of my townhouse. "I'll see you tomorrow then! And thanks again for organizing that concert. The Johansens were thrilled with it."

"I thought the kids did pretty well, didn't you?" he said.

"Not really," I said in a low voice. "But it was worth the pain."

I went inside. Mom and Dad had just come back from skiing.

"Hey there, stranger," Dad said. "All finished with your baby-sitting?"

"All finished," I said.

"Your mom's making a pot of hot chocolate," Dad said. "Will you join us?"

"Sounds good," I said.

Mary-Kate appeared at the top of the stairs. "Ashley! You're finally home!" she cried. "I have big news. Gigantic news!"

111

"What?" I asked. I ran upstairs.

"If you want that coffee, we'll keep it warm for you down here!" Dad called after me.

I hurried into Mary-Kate's room. Coffee could wait. "What's the big news?" I asked.

"You were right, Ashley. Bill finally admitted it. He *is* the prince!"

I fell back onto her bed. Even though I'd suspected it all along, it was still a shock. "He admitted it? What did he say?"

Mary-Kate told me about the whole conversation. While I listened, I thought about what Nate had found out about the prince. The newspaper articles had made him sound so arrogant and spoiled. And hardly a one-girl guy.

Is Bill really like that? I wondered. I hoped it wasn't true. It *couldn't* be true, I decided. Nate was right. The newspapers were wrong. We'd spent enough time with Bill to know what kind of person he was.

"Ever since he admitted it, I feel weird," Mary-Kate said. "I used to just enjoy being around him. But now I'm always thinking, 'He's the prince. And he'll go home to his tiny little country in Europe and I'll never see him again.' And if I do, things will never be normal anyway."

"You know what, Mary-Kate?" I said. "Don't think about it. We're going to the fab Christmas

Eve party tomorrow night as guests of the Prince of Montavan! That's exactly what we hoped would happen when we got here a week ago. So—mission accomplished! Enjoy it while you can!"

"You're right," she said. "It's just not the way I imagined it would be. . . ."

"Who knows?" I said. "Maybe it will be even better!"

chapter thirteen

"**R**ight this way, sir." The host led Bill, me, Nate, and Ashley to a table by the tall picture windows in the ballroom. On the way we passed Mom and Dad, who sat at another table with friends they'd met on the slopes.

"Don't get too comfortable, girls," Dad warned. "I expect to have at least one dance with each of you before the night's over."

"It's a deal, Dad," I said.

We sat down and looked out over the ski slopes lined with colored lights.

"This is definitely the best table in the room," Ashley whispered to me. "We'll have a great view of the torchlight skiers at midnight."

I felt like a princess in my pink silk dress, with Bill holding my hand. The Christmas Eve Gala, at last. The room bustled with beautifully dressed people, and was decorated like an enchanted forest. Candles and tiny lights flickered, and a tall Christmas tree decorated with antique ornaments stood in the center of the room.

A waiter arrived and filled our glasses with sparkling cider. Bill raised his glass.

"I'd like to make a toast," he said. "To Mary-Kate and Ashley. Thank you for making this Christmas very special."

We sipped our cider. Then Ashley raised her glass again.

"I'd like to make a toast, too," she said. "To Bill—thank you for bringing us to this beautiful party. And to Nate—thanks for all your help with the Johansens. Especially yesterday. You're a hero."

"Cheers!" we cried, and clinked glasses.

We went to the buffet, where they served everything from turkey and roast beef to caviar and lobster.

"Is everything to your satisfaction, sir?" the waiter asked Bill.

He nodded. "Everything is fantastic," he said. The resort staff all paid special attention to Bill. Being with him really did feel like being with royalty. And I had to admit it wasn't bad. Not bad at all.

The party started heating up. The lights came up over the stage and everyone started to cheer.

Then three guys and two girls, dressed in glam rock clothes, took the stage.

"Ladies and gentlemen," an announcer said. "The Snowbeam Resort is proud to present Cargo!"

The crowd cheered and whistled. The band started playing their latest hit, and people flooded the dance floor.

Bill took my hand. "Come on, Mary-Kate. I want to get you out there before your father snatches you away."

Ashley turned to Nate. "Dance?" she asked.

Nate blushed. "I'm not a great dancer," he said.

"Oh, come on." Ashley grabbed his hand and dragged him to his feet. "I'll bet you're better than you think."

We joined the crowd on the dance floor. I stared at the band, so close I could touch them. I couldn't believe I was actually dancing to Cargo, live! They normally played in big arenas, but here they were, playing just for us, a small group of maybe a hundred.

"This next song is our version of Elvis's 'Blue Christmas,'" the lead singer announced.

The band launched into the slow song. Dad tapped Bill on the shoulder. "May I cut in?" he asked. "Don't worry, I won't keep her too long."

Bill stepped aside, and Dad and I danced. Bill went and got Mom and led her to the dance floor.

He's so sweet, I thought as I watched him dance with Mom. *This is such a wonderful Christmas. I've got my family with me, and a gorgeous guy who really likes me. I can't remember when I've ever been happier.*

If only it could last!

❁

Nate was kind of a goofy dancer, but not bad, really. He was stiff and shy at first, but once he got warmed up, he could really go.

I danced a slow song with Dad and then the band ripped into some of their harder stuff. Nate and I burned up the dance floor. When Cargo left the stage, Nate said, "I'm not ready to stop yet!"

"Me neither," I agreed. "But I do need about three glasses of water before I can hit the dance floor again."

We rested at our table for a few minutes. Nate and I had something to eat and lots of water.

"I'm ready to go," Nate said. "When's that band coming back?"

A man in a red sequined tuxedo jacket and slicked black hair took the stage. "Merry Christmas, ladies and gentlemen," he said in a European accent. "I am Armando. While that wimpy rock band takes a break, I'm going to teach you some *real* dance moves."

He cued the DJ, and a funky old song from the

early 60s started playing. "This one is called the watusi!" Armando called out. He started wiggling his hips and waving his arms around. Everybody joined in.

"Come on," Nate said. "That looks like fun."

We ran out onto the dance floor and started watusi-ing. Soon we were twisting, frugging, and jerking like pros. Nate was hilarious. His arms and legs were long and spindly, so every dance looked extra goofy when he did it.

"All right, Nate!" I shouted. People circled around us to watch. Nate was letting all his shyness drop away and really getting into it. It was so good to see him having fun.

"You! In the bow tie!" Armando called, pointing at Nate. "Up on the table. I want everyone to see your fabulous swim!"

Nate hopped up on the nearest table. He waved his arms like a swimmer. Then he held his nose and wiggled up and down.

The crowd clapped and cheered him on. Mary-Kate and Bill were laughing and clapping, too. Then everyone spread out on the floor, dancing with their partners.

I jumped up on the table and danced with Nate. I glanced at the stage. Armando had stopped dancing. He was staring at Nate, his jaw hanging open. What was up with him?

Armando ran off the stage.

"Your Highness!" Armando said, clutching Nate's hand. "It's you!"

Nate looked at Armando and blinked. Then he jumped down off the table. I jumped down, too. The music kept playing and the crowd kept dancing. They had no idea what was going on.

"Prince Stephen!" Armando said. "Don't you remember? It's me, Armando!"

Prince Stephen? I thought. *Your Highness? What was Armando talking about?*

"You've made a mistake," I said to Armando. "This isn't Stephen. This is Nate." I pointed toward Bill. "*That's* Stephen."

But Nate broke into a grin. "Hey, Armando!" he said. He gave Armando a hug. "It's great to see you again!"

"It's great to see you, too, Your Highness," Armando said. "I haven't seen you since you were a little boy! But as soon as I got a good look at you up on that table, I knew it was you!"

I stared at Nate. He suddenly looked shy. "Nate, what is he talking about?" I asked.

"Well, um—this is an old family friend. . . ." Nate began.

"I worked in the royal palace!" Armando said. "I was on Queen Anne's staff, planning special events. I planned the prince's sixth birthday party myself!" He pinched Nate's cheek and added, "Look how handsome you are!"

"But—" I looked over at Bill again. Wasn't *he* the prince? He saw us talking to Armando. He grabbed Mary-Kate's hand and hurried over.

"Hey," Bill said. "Is everything okay here?"

"It's all right, Bill," Nate said. "It's just—"

"Armando says that Nate is the Prince of Montavan," I told Bill and Mary-Kate. "Is that true?"

Bill looked from Mary-Kate to Nate and back to me.

"It's okay, Bill," Nate said. "It's out now. You can tell them."

"Tell us what?" Mary-Kate cried.

"The truth," Nate said.

chapter fourteen

I stared at Bill, totally confused. "Bill, what is going on?" I demanded. "You told me *you* were the prince!"

Bill looked uncomfortable. "I'm sorry, Mary-Kate. I can explain—"

"Uh-oh," Armando said. "Did I say something wrong? Me and my big mouth!"

"It's all right, Armando," Nate said. "These are my friends. I can trust them."

"Trust us with what?" Ashley eyed Armando as he slipped away.

Nate looked Ashley in the eye. "I am Prince Stephen," he said.

Ashley gripped my hand. My head was reeling, and I knew hers must be, too.

"But . . . how can that be?" Ashley said. "Bill said *he* was the prince!"

"I know," Nate admitted. "But I'm the real

Prince Stephen. Nate was just the name I used so no one would guess my true identity."

"It worked," Ashley said.

I was confused and angry all at once. It was slowly becoming clear that Bill had lied to me. *But why?* Furious, I turned on him. "If he's the prince, who are you?"

"Bill is my bodyguard," Nate, or Prince Stephen, explained. "Don't be mad at him, Mary-Kate. He only lied to you to protect me. He had to. It's part of his job."

I stared at Bill, waiting for his explanation. I just hoped it would be the truth this time.

"I'm sorry, Mary-Kate," Bill said. "My job is to protect Stephen. He was only safe as long as no one knew who he was. And it was going so well! I could even give him a little privacy. But then Stephen told me that Ashley suspected something. And she was getting close to the truth. So when you asked me if I was the prince, I lied—to throw Ashley off the trail and to help Stephen stay anonymous."

"I was having the best time of my life," Stephen said. It was hard not to think of him as Nate. And very hard to see him as a prince. "If everyone knew I was the prince, I never would have been able to go caroling or take care of the Johansen kids . . . Bill didn't want to lie to you, Mary-Kate. He did it for me."

"Please forgive me, Mary-Kate," Bill added. "I was dying to tell you the truth. But I couldn't, for Stephen's sake."

He held my hand and looked into my eyes, and I could tell he was sincere. My anger faded away. He was so loyal to Stephen, and such a good friend . . . it only made me like him more.

And then I remembered—I never wanted Bill to be the prince in the first place! All I wanted was a normal relationship with him. And now I had my wish! "I forgive you, Bill," I said. "Actually, I'm glad you're not the prince."

"So am I," Bill said. "Now I can be your boyfriend!"

The DJ played a slow song, and Bill led me to the dance floor. I had a feeling Ashley had some things to work out with her baby-sitting buddy, the prince.

❈

"In a way, I was right all along," I said, trying to understand what was going on. "Bill *was* hiding something. It just wasn't exactly what I thought."

"Ashley, I know this is a shock," Stephen said. He led me to an empty table and we sat down.

"I still don't get it," I said. "How can you be the prince? You never have any money!"

"I usually don't need it," he explained. "When people know I'm the prince, they hardly ever let me pay for anything! And if I do need cash, Bill carries it for me."

"But what about all the evidence I saw?" I asked. I just couldn't see Nate as a prince, no matter how hard I tried. It wouldn't sink into my brain. "I saw Bill's jacket in the prince's suite."

"That's right," he said. "We're staying in the suite together. And Bill is the one who orders that weird sandwich and milkshake every night. I'd never be able to sleep if I ate that before I went to bed."

"What about all that stuff you read to me about arrogant Prince Stephen, out on the town with a different girl every night? You even said he was tall!"

He shrugged. "I made it up to throw you off the trail. But you wouldn't be thrown. You're very persistent."

"So when the ski patrol stopped us, Bill must have told them that *you* were the prince," I said. "And I misinterpreted it. I misinterpreted everything!"

My head was still reeling, and to make it worse, a wave of embarrassment washed over me. *What had I done? Why hadn't I seen it?*

I had the Prince of Montavan chasing after a bunch of bratty kids all day. And I had paid him minimum wage to do it!

I shut my eyes and shook my head. I had even

asked him to investigate himself! I felt like such an idiot!

"Nate—I mean, Your Highness—I'm so sorry," I stammered. "I can't believe all the stuff I made you do. You even cleaned up after Soupy!"

He looked hurt. "But I wanted to do that stuff—all of it!" he protested. "I wanted to baby-sit with you. I had a great time!" He turned my head and forced me to look him in the eye. It was hard, I was so embarrassed. "I'm still the same guy I was ten minutes ago."

I smiled. "I'm glad," I said. "Because that guy is really great."

"Ladies and gentlemen, it's almost midnight!" Armando called. "The torchlight ceremony will begin in five minutes!"

"Come on, Ashley," Stephen said. "It's Christmas! This is what we came for. Let's forget all about this crazy stuff and just have fun."

"All right," I agreed. He took my hand and led me to the window. Bill and Mary-Kate stood beside us. We watched the skiers ski down the mountain with their torches.

"It's midnight!" Bill called. "Merry Christmas, everyone!"

"Merry Christmas!" we all shouted. Stephen handed me a cup of hot cocoa and we clinked our mugs together.

"To a great new year," he said.

"To friendship," I said.

We sipped our cocoa. "There's one more thing I'm confused about," I told him. "I can't stop thinking of you as Nate. But that isn't your name. So what should I call you?"

"How about His Highness Prince Stephen Norbert Henrik Paul of Montavan?" he joked. I smiled. "Just call me what Bill and my other friends call me—Steve."

"All right, Steve," I said. "It will take some getting used to. And so will thinking of you as a prince."

"Don't think of me as a prince," Steve said. "Think of me as I really am—your friend."

We gathered around the Christmas tree and sang carols. The candlelight glowed on all the warm, happy faces. Mom and Dad sang together, arm in arm. Mary-Kate and Bill snuggled happily. Stephen stood beside me, singing one of the songs he taught to the Johansens—but much better, of course.

This really was a dream holiday, I thought happily. *Merry Christmas!*

Find out what happens next in

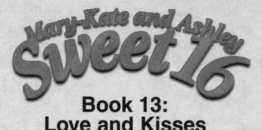

Book 13:
Love and Kisses

I took a deep breath and knocked on the half-open door marked C.K. FEIN, FEATURES EDITOR. It was my first day of work at *Girlz Magazine* and my stomach was in knots. I poked my head into the office. "Hello? Ms. Fein?"

Ms. Fein sat hunched over her keyboard, typing furiously.

She didn't say anything.

I cleared my throat. "It's me, Mary-Kate Olsen."

Without looking up, Ms. Fein waved one hand toward the seat across from her desk. It had a pile of books and magazines on it. I moved them to the floor and sat down.

Somehow Ms. Fein wasn't what I pictured a glamorous magazine editor would look like. She was dressed in a wrinkled gray suit and had pencils stuck in her curly brown hair.

Finally, she stopped typing and looked at me.

"Call me CK," she said. "Do you want some coffee? How did you find out about this job? What grade are you in?"

"No coffee for me, thanks. I'm a sophomore at Bayside High. Ms. Barbour told me about this job. She's my English teacher. She also manages the school Website, which I—"

"Oh, yes, yes, yes," CK cut in. "I have some of your writing samples right here. I enjoyed this one about high school cliques. And the one about surviving freshman year was very good, too. You have talent."

Wow! A real magazine editor was telling me that I had talent! I wanted to jump up and cheer, but I knew that wouldn't be too cool. I couldn't wait to tell my sister, Ashley, though.

"Thank you," I said to CK. "I think that my experience writing for the school Website will make me a—"

"Yes, yes, yes," CK cut in again. She picked up her desk calendar and riffled through it. "We're putting together our February Valentine's Day issue right now." She stared at me over the top of her purple glasses. "Quick! Give me three ideas for Valentine's Day stories"—she looked at her watch—"starting now!"

"Ummm . . . " Suddenly, I couldn't think of a single idea!

Was I about to lose the job before I even started?

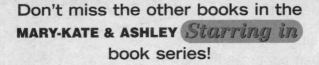

Coming soon...A new mary-kateandashley 2004 calendar!

Own The Hit Series on DVD and Video!